Ride The Mountain

Patrick Gooch

First published in 2024 by Blossom Spring Publishing
Ride The Mountain Copyright © 2024 Patrick Gooch
ISBN 978-1-7385023-1-8
E: admin@blossomspringpublishing.com
W: www.blossomspringpublishing.com
All rights reserved under International Copyright Law.
Contents and/or cover may not be reproduced in whole
or in part without the express written consent
of the publisher.
Names, characters, places and incidents are either products
of the author's imagination or are used fictitiously.

CHAPTER ONE

Bolshaya Dmitrovka Street, Moscow

He looked in the mirror and adjusted the knot of his tie. Every aspect of his appearance must be absolutely right.

Smoothing his hair, his gaze shifted to the man standing behind him.

"How do I look, Alexei?"

"OK...except your trouser zip needs attention."

A hand involuntarily grabbed at his midriff. Then a slight smile. "You joke, my friend. But this will be the last time you do so. Do you understand?"

"If you say so, Leoni."

He stared intently into the mirror, turning his head first one way, then the other. "I'm getting a double chin. You didn't tell me I was getting a double chin. I thought you were my personal adviser. Perhaps I should invite someone else to do your job."

A comment made all too regularly to keep Alexei Sokolov on his toes.

Leoni Tupolev twisted to look at his body profile. He was sixty-two years old, his figure enhanced by wearing a man's deep girdle to hide the early suggestion of a bulge.

Although of medium height, in addition to colouring

his hair, when photographed, Tupolev always insisted cameras be pointed slightly upwards to enforce the impression he was taller.

With one last glance, he said. "Right, I am ready. Lead me to them."

Sokolov opened the door, and stood back to allow Tupolev to pass.

He walked purposely along the red carpet lining the corridor and came to a halt before large double doors. Opened by attendants on the other side, Leoni Tupolev entered the chamber on Bolshaya Dmitrovka Street to give his first speech as President to the Federation Council.

"So. . .what did you think? Was it OK?"

Sokolov did not rush to reply, to be effusive with praise: that might have signalled the wrong message. Though, in fact, it would have been the right one. For Tupolev had not delivered the telling declaration that political power now resided in his hands. The speech had hinted, but never spelt out that the new President should be regarded as the supreme authority on all matters of state.

They were in the President's quarters in the Kremlin's Senate building. Sokolov was standing one side of the opulent desk, while Tupolev lounged in a comfortable, leather chair on the other.

"Yes, it was fine. They now know who is in charge. Who wrote the speech. . .Dimitri? Perhaps it could have been a little more emphatic. . .but that can come later."

Tupolev's eyes narrowed.

"Say what you mean, my friend. That's what I pay you

for."

"I'm saying it was fine. In fact, on reflection, it was probably exactly the right approach. You had them guessing. . .what is the new guy actually telling us. Not dictatorial, for you kept repeating the phrase `working together for the common good`. But, at the same time, leaving them with few illusions you had the last word."

Tupolev started swinging to and fro in his chair. A sure sign of his displeasure.

"I wanted more than that! They should have got the clear message this office makes all the decisions. . .not them. Get Dimitri in here. I want a letter sent to all one hundred and eighty-seven members of the Council!"

Alexei Sokolov returned to his apartment on Davykovskaya Street just after ten that evening.

He poured himself a whisky, and switched on `Moscow 24`, to catch the latest news. But there was nothing to concern him. Stretching out on a settee, Sokolov reviewed the day`s events.

He had worked alongside Tupolev since he was a junior member of the Moscow Duma. Back then he was approachable, listened to reason. But he had changed.

In those days they were like brothers, sharing and solving problems together. Alexei Sokolov was more than Leonie`s personal adviser, he was his confidant, his helpmate. Always on hand, ready to boost his confidence when down; to share, albeit discreetly, in his triumphs.

Now the man was impossible.

He toyed with Sokolov. One day promising him the role of Chief of Staff of the Presidential Executive Office; the next, likely dispensing with his services as the whim took him.

Should I let him choose someone else to take my place he wondered. Experienced in working closely with those in high office he would have little difficulty finding another job. But would it pay as well? Moreover, Sokolov would lose the use of the grace and favour apartment in the Edelweiss luxury tower block, and the GAZ Volga car that went with the presidential adviser`s post.

Just as light dawned the phone rang.

"Alexei, come over to the compound. I want you to do something for me."

"OK, Leonie, give me half an hour."

Alexei showered, dressed hurriedly and fifteen minutes later drove out the car park turning north-west for Route A -106. He was heading for the President`s Moscow home off the Rublyovo-Uspenskoye Highway.

Even though Leoni Tupolev had seemingly won a landslide victory in the race for the presidency, many queried his achievement. There were suggestions of wilful manipulation, underhand dealing, and intimidation. Though nothing appeared in the media: neither the Russian newspapers nor TV stations openly voiced their true opinions. The Russian constitution provided for freedom of speech; but, all too often journalists were forced to tread a wary path when reporting controversial issues.

However, with today`s ease of communication, there was nothing to prevent information being leaked to the outside world; and revelations about the more questionable aspects of the Kremlin hierarchy would appear in the western press and social media; and, predictably, such shortcomings found their way back to the Russian people.

One very sensitive item that aroused comment even in the Russian papers, and reflected badly on the then president was his Residence at Cape Idokopas on the Black Sea.

It was a large Italianate-style complex at Gelendzhik Krasnodar Krai north of Sochi, and was reported to have cost between six hundred million and a billion dollars, siphoned off from funds destined for medical projects.

Even though those working on the site were sworn to secrecy, it was not long before its secrets seeped out. Photographs illustrating the opulence of the palace were taken by a construction worker, and first appeared on the WikiLeaks website.

Such was the level of public indignation, to avoid constant innuendo appearing in the media, the complex was sold — on paper — to Alexander Ponomarenko, a Russian businessman. He claimed the property was now his holiday home; but security was still high, and barbed wire and guard dogs were employed around the clock to keep the inquisitive at bay.

"Let us go into the inner sanctum."

Tupolev led the way through the outer office, manned by a male receptionist and two bodyguards from the Federalnaya Sluzhba Bezopasnosti, Russia's federal security service. One of them jumped to his feet and opened the tall double doors.

Tupolev marched into the wood-panelled salon, past the long conference table, towards his desk in front of which was an extension for more intimate discussions.

"Sit there, Alexei, opposite me," said the President, pulling back a chair. "Now, it`s quite straightforward," he continued, "I want you to organise my visit to the compound by the Black Sea."

"As you wish, Leoni. Just let me know the dates and I`ll brief Ludmilla. She usually organises your travel arrangements."

"This time I want you to do it. No one else."

Alexei raised an eyebrow.

Tupolev said casually. "By the way, I`m taking Olga with me. Obviously, I want you to make sure no one learns where I`m going, and who I`m with. Do you understand me?"

The enormity of the task hit Sokolov.

Not only did the tide of ill-feeling persist about the Cape Idokopas residence — few were convinced it was owned by Ponomarenko. But to take Olga Petrova, the President`s mistress instead of his wife, was courting disaster.

"Are you sure, Leoni?" queried Sokolov. "Aren`t you taking too much of a risk?"

Tupolev smiled. "I`m not taking any risks, Alexei. . .you are. Let`s see what you can do to justify your presence as my personal aide."

The meaning was all too obvious.

CHAPTER TWO

Bischofshofen, Austria

I was close to the barrier surrounding the runout.

Around me a lively crowd in brightly-coloured, warm clothing cheered each skier as they leapt from the ramp and floated down the hill.

Soon it would be Anatoly's turn. I could see him edging across the narrow starting board. When ready he would centre his skis in the tracking, hurtle down the slope and launch himself into space at over ninety kilometres an hour.

Sheer lunacy.

Nevertheless, he was in the lead after his first jump of a hundred and thirty-five metres. If he could match that in the second round he would, surely, be crowned the Four Hills champion.

Personally, I have never understood jumpers, or 'eagles' as they are known. Not only is the sport highly dangerous, like jockeys they are lightly-built, watch everything they eat, and wear what appears next to nothing in bitter weather.

And the day was bitingly cold, even for January.

As the name suggests, the Four Hills Tournament requires competitors to throw themselves down four mountains all in the space of ten days. From the 28th of December to the 6th of January each year, fifty of the world`s top jumpers congregate at Oberstdorf and Garmisch-Partenkirchen in southern Germany. Thereafter, they cross into Austria for the next two venues at Innsbruck and Bischofshofen.

I stamped the ground to resurrect some semblance of life in my feet. I had only been at the Paul-Ausserleitner-Schanze ski jump for half an hour, yet I was shivering. How the more ardent fans stood for hours to cheer on their favourites I`ll never know.

I first met Anatoly Vasiliev in a wine bar in Sochi, during the 2014 Winter Olympics. I was in the British team, competing in the Downhill. He was Russia`s leading ski-jumper.

I had introduced myself in halting Russian, only to find that Anatoly spoke impeccable English. There was an immediate rapport: over the years it developed into a close friendship. We visited each other`s homes, met whenever we could, and kept in regular contact.

Why I was a spectator at the Paul-Ausserleitner-Schanze ski jump was due to a chance meeting in Salzburg Airport. I was heading for Kitzbühel, Anatoly, and his team, were off to Bischofshofen for the final leg of the Tournament.

"Adam. . .Adam Livesey!" I remember him calling out.

I turned and there was this slight figure rushing towards me, a huge grin on his face. We clasped each other in a manly embrace. However, breaking apart, Anatoly`s voice took on a worrying tone. "Adam, am I glad to see you! Walk with me towards the exit and the team bus. I think I may need your help. I can't go into detail now, but can you come over to Bischofshofen, and I'll explain everything."

"Well, not immediately, Anatoly. I'm preparing for the Streif, the Downhill in Kitzbühel. For us downhillers it's one of the main runs of the season. Perhaps, I could meet you later?"

He bit his lip. "This is urgent, Adam...really urgent." His voice conveyed concern.

"Tell me what's troubling you, Anatoly."

"I can't say much now. But I was in Lucerne forty-eight hours ago, and witnessed something which, on reflection, I clearly should not have seen."

He glanced around. "I was staying at the Grand Hotel on Haldenstrasse, visiting my insurance company, sorting out one or two personal details. When I came out the hotel this morning I glanced across the road, and..."

"Come on, Anatoly! We're ready to go!" called one of the team.

"Look, I'll come to Bischofshofen the day after tomorrow...is that all right?"

He grabbed my hand. "Thank you, Adam. I knew I could rely on you."

And then it was Anatoly's turn.

He sat on the starting board waiting for a brief lull in the chill crosswinds. Suddenly, the wind eased, his coach signalled with a wave of the arm, Anatoly leapt forward, careering down the slope.

All eyes were on the solitary skier speeding towards the brink of the ramp. One well-executed jump, and the title would be his.

There was grace in his flight very few could match. It was as he assumed the v-style, with the forward tips of his skis thrust outwards, that it happened.

One moment Anatoly was soaring like a bird. . .the next, his left ski fell away, and he was tumbling from the sky.

The cheering gave way to screaming before the once-boisterous crowd fell deathly quiet.

Anatoly hit the hill, and the remaining ski fell away. Nothing could halt his headlong descent, arms, legs flung at increasingly acute angles, his torso battered as he was unmercifully tossed to one side. Even before he had come to a halt I had clambered over the barrier and was running towards him. The dread of what I might behold churning my stomach. I passed his coach also heading towards the now still body.

The medical team was there before us. Anatoly was already being lifted onto a stretcher. I walked with them to a waiting helicopter, and without being questioned, his coach and I climbed in.

While I was gently holding his hand, his eyes opened.

"Adam," he whispered. "Come closer."

I knelt beside the stretcher. His voice was fading. All he could manage were two words, `microswitch` and `UPS`.

Suddenly, his back arched in overwhelming pain. Perhaps a blessed relief, with one long sigh, Anatoly Vasiliev lapsed into unconsciousness on the way to the hospital.

What had a microswitch to do with United Parcel Service, the international delivery company, I wondered.

CHAPTER THREE

At the Cardinal Schwarzenburg Hospital, Vasiliev's coach and I had been ushered into a small side room. A television was soundlessly relaying the news, and a few moments later the skiing accident was featured. It portrayed the disaster in slow motion, and suddenly the cause of my friend's accident became much clearer.

A few seconds into the jump the adjustable bar controlling the height of the left heel appeared to come away from the boot, causing him to lose balance. With arms and legs flailing, Anatoly plummeted down the slope coming to a broken halt against the side barrier.

The video showed the emergency medical team rushing towards the inert figure. I could see from their faces little could be done for the ski-jumper. Lifted onto the stretcher they had hurriedly carried him to a helicopter, its blades already turning.

I turned away from the broadcast.

"How the hell could that come loose? Where was the tie?" I exploded.

"I don't know," he said in fractured English. "I check the bindings, the skis, everything."

"Well you didn't do a very good job," I shouted. "You

might have cost a man his life!"

Rage was consuming me. It was obvious he hadn`t been sufficiently diligent. About to vent my anger further, the door opened and one of the paramedics attending the jumps appeared.

"I am sorry, gentlemen, Herr Vasiliev died a few minutes ago. We did our best, but his injuries were too severe."

Still fuming I took a taxi back to Bischofshofen.

Numb from the loss of a dear friend, a mixture of grief, shock and anger overwhelmed me. In the hire car, I remained in the driver`s seat for more than an hour pondering on how such an accident could have occurred.

The coach was adamant he had examined Vasiliev`s equipment the night before, even double-checking everything before the second jump. So what had caused the failure of the heel bar? I also realised that with four other Russian jumpers taking part in the Four Hills tournament, their coach would have been stretched to oversee everyone`s equipment. So, was it just an unfortunate mishap and no one was really to blame?

I started the engine and drove out the car park. Turning onto Route B311, I headed for Kitzbühel. During the ninety-minute journey I mused on the problem confronting professional skiers. This season`s schedule had been turned upside down by the lack of snow. Venues had been changed, competitions cancelled, major events put back in the hope conditions on the slopes would improve. And now a death to blight an already depressing year.

***

"Something must be done. . .and done immediately!" declared the elder of the two men. They were alone on the open deck at the stern of the Stadt Luzern, a paddle steamer that sailed Lake Lucerne. The changeable weather persuading other passengers not to stray from the comfort of the salons.

He had arrived that morning. A waiting limousine had collected him from the airport and driven to the quay where the craft was being readied. His companion was waiting by the boarding ramp.

The timing was perfect. Last to go on board, they now watched the ship's wake as it headed towards Vitznau.

"I want to be rid of this fellow Livesey, do you hear!" declared the speaker, gripping the handrail to steady himself against the bracing wind. Normally, when in Lucerne, he followed a set routine. First, an excellent meal prepared by the chef on the lovingly-restored Stadt Luzern. Thereafter, he would spend time fulfilling his role as the CEO of the company before visiting the Banque Senlis et Fils, checking accounts, boxes in the strong room, and reviewing the organisation's investments.

However, before taking his customary table, he wanted to make sure his companion would carry out his demands.

"But you don't know Vasiliev told him anything. My people have kept a close watch on him for the past few days. If he knew he would certainly have reacted by now," his companion pointed out.

"You don't understand, I am not prepared to take that risk. Such uncertainty does not sit well with me. Whether he was party or not to Vasiliev's chance sighting, I want *him dealt with."*

"If you say so."

"I do say so! It should be easy enough, a man of your talents."

"The same fee paid in two instalments? Half now, the rest on completion."

"Of course. Now, let me introduce you to the work of one of the finest chefs in Switzerland."

CHAPTER FOUR

I met Josh Finden, my agent, in the bar of the Hotel Schweizerhof.

The bluff, hearty Canadian, once a downhill racer, was a larger-than-life character. Besides advising me and plotting which races best served my development as a downhill skier, he also guided the future of a number of athletes across various skiing disciplines.

He now lived permanently in Europe, and had gathered around him a school of retired skiers, who sought out and trained emerging men and women likely become the next generation of professional skiers.

'Get them when they are young', was his mantra, and seemingly it worked. Josh had established his organisation in Lucerne, and currently had a workforce of about thirty people, evenly split between administrators, public relations and trainers.

Typical of the Finden group, rooms had been booked for his charges in the hotel, which was located at the foot of the Streif downhill course, and opposite the lower terminus of the Hahnenkamm cable car.

As I approached he got to his feet. I'm six one, but he towered over me.

"Adam," he called. "It`s sure good to see you."

He shook my hand, peering closely at me. "You don`t look so hot. Were you at Bischofshofen?"

I nodded.

"Gee, I`m sorry. Anatoly was a great guy. When`s the funeral?"

"Next week. . .during the Streif."

"Hmm, what are you going to do? Ski or attend the service?"

"I had thought to go to Moscow, Josh, to forget about skiing. But when I spoke to Anatoly`s father he informed me only family members would be attending the funeral. He didn`t hold with his son pursuing such a dangerous sport. In as many words, he told me none of his skiing friends would be welcome. He didn`t want to be reminded of what caused his son`s death."

"So, you`ll be competing in the Streif?"

"I guess so. . .but I`ve been thinking. The preliminaries don`t start for another few days. If you agree, I`d like to take a brief time out and check with Todd Stewart, the British team performance coach at their training camp in Tignes."

Finden shrugged. "Up to you, my boy. As you say, we have a couple of days before practising begins in earnest. If you want, sure, link up with your home squad."

In truth, I wanted a break from the demands Josh might impose in the build-up to the Streif. I was not of the mindset to plunge straight in to preparing for the event.

I drove the hire car to Innsbruck and caught a late evening flight to Geneva. The Hertz desk provided me with a vehicle, and the satnav guided me to Tignes.

I had booked a room in the Hôtel Le Refuge, and rested briefly on the bed before unpacking my overnight bag. I awoke with a start. My watch showed it was three o'clock in the morning. Unfortunately, thereafter, I slept fitfully until it was time for a shower. A cold thirty seconds brought me to my senses, and after breakfast I strolled through Tignes looking for somewhere to buy sunglasses. Leaving Kitzbühel when it was dark, I had forgotten to bring mine with me. That unthinking lapse cost me a hundred and twenty Euros.

It was a clear, crisp day, the sun bright in the morning sky when I made my way to the Résidence Bonhomme Neige, which housed the British team.

As I came to the entrance the door opened and Jeff Rivers, our slalom specialist, called. "Now there's a sight for sore eyes. We were wondering if you would put in an appearance. It's good to see you, Adam."

"So, everyone OK? Nothing broken I hope."

"One or two strains, bruises which the physio is treating, nothing of any consequence," Jeff remarked. "Though a few of them are getting stir crazy. Todd's regime of no late nights, no booze, no fraternising with the locals, is making some a little boisterous. But that's to be expected. Anyway, come in, say hello to everyone."

He led me towards the lounge, where there seemed to be a number of raised voices and much laughter. Jeff was reaching to open the door when it flew open and a fellow shot past us, and hared down the corridor. In hot pursuit was another figure who misjudged speed, distance and angle and cannoned straight into me.

I went backwards heavily, hitting the opposite wall, followed by a second battering encounter by the individual falling on top of me.

Stunned, I lay still for a moment while my attacker got slowly to a kneeling position.

"Oh, God, Adam, I`m sorry," she cried.

I opened an eye. It was Suzanna Bancroft, the women`s team captain.

I sat up slowly. "You could at least have done a simple stem turn to miss me," I muttered. I put my hand in a pocket and drew out the broken sunglasses. "Well, these didn`t last long. I bought them only ten minutes ago."

The tableau of me sitting against a corridor wall with Suzanna kneeling beside me must have looked strange to Todd Stewart as he came through the main door.

"Hello, Adam. Getting acquainted with Suzanna? I like to see team members exchanging ideas on how minimise injury when sliding down the slopes on their arse. Presumably, this is a practical demonstration?"

"Very amusing, Todd," I remarked, getting slowly to my feet and gingerly feeling myself. "Your leading Super G skier, and team captain, just knocked me off my feet. I`m about to check for damage, other than ruining a perfectly good pair of sunglasses. I think everything is OK. Ouch! I spoke too soon."

When I lifted my right arm above my head, pain shot down the side of my body.

Todd`s bemused face suddenly changed to deadly serious.

"Quick. . .Jeff, get Phyllis! Tell her it`s urgent! Where shall we take him?"

"To my room. . .it`s just along the corridor," declared Suzanna.

"Look, it's only a twinge. . .it will be all right." I said.

"Maybe. . .maybe not. We'll make sure when Phyllis, our physio, gives you the once over," Todd replied, half carrying me into Suzanna's room and dropping me on the bed.

A round, rosy-cheeked woman of middle years appeared in the doorway.

"Jeff said it was urgent, Todd. What seems to be the trouble?"

"You haven't met Adam Livesey, our downhill racer. He had a run-in with Suzanna, and came off worse. Every time he lifts his right arm pain shoots up his side. Put him back together for me, there's a dear."

"Right, everyone out while I take a look," she declared, shooing Suzanna, Todd and Jeff from the room.

Phyllis spent the next twenty minutes stretching and massaging my side and shoulder.

Finally, she stepped back.

"Well, if you are anything of a downhill racer, you'll probably suffer more than that during the season. Just give yourself a rest. The bruising will come out and will hurt a bit. Just don't do anything strenuous for the next few days."

"I don't have that luxury. I have to be back in Kitzbühel tomorrow to begin qualifying for the Streif."

"Do you now?" she murmured. "How are you travelling?"

"By road to Geneva, a flight to Innsbruck, then by road again to Kitzbühel."

"Mm. . .that will involve a lot of driving," Phyllis muttered. "There'd be no improvement if you drive yourself, it would be a strain on your deltoid and intercostal muscles. As it is, I wouldn't recommend you taking part in the downhill. Attempting such a demanding run after two long drives is asking for trouble."

Without knocking, Suzanna marched in, and plumped down on the bed beside me.

"Ouch. . .that looks nasty," she said staring at the bruising as it darkened.

"Do you mind," I said testily. "I could have been without the rest of my clothes on!"

She shrugged. "That`s OK, I wouldn`t have been embarrassed."

"Perhaps not, but I would," I retorted.

"Did you know Adam is taking part in the Streif, Suzanna?" Phyllis remarked. "By rights, he shouldn`t even contemplate putting on skis for the next four or five days. But he is adamant. So someone has got to drive him to the airport in Geneva, and thereafter, from Innsbruck to Kitzbühel."

Phyllis looked at Suzanna expectantly.

"I`m sure we can ask someone to do that. One of the team not immediately on call," she mused.

Phyllis looked at her sharply. "Like you, for instance. After all, you were responsible for his injuries."

For a moment Suzanna looked nonplussed.

Then, hesitatingly, she murmured. "I suppose I could. . .I`m not skiing for a while, just exercising, doing gym work. I`ll go and speak with Todd."

She jumped off the bed and made for the door, pulling it shut behind her.

"I happen to know her schedule," grinned Phyllis. "She caused the accident; she should at least try to make amends. Anyway, she`s not competing until next week."

Five minutes later Suzanna was back.

"I`ve spoken with Todd, and that`s OK. As long as

I'm back by the weekend."

"Thanks," I said. "I'll speak to the car hire company and nominate you as driver."

"Right," she said breezily. "And Todd wants a word with you after lunch."

"Do you mind slowing down?" I said, with something like a plea in my voice. "The bends are throwing me around, and the seat belt is cutting into my side."

The D902 road out of Tignes is a switchback of twists and turns. One minute you are climbing, the next dropping down into wooded valleys. If she skis like she drives, I thought, she probably throws herself down the slopes, and ploughs through the gates. More determination than finesse.

"Right ho," Suzanna said breezily, taking her foot marginally off the accelerator. But only briefly; I had to mention it a number of times before we reached the Mont Blanc Tunnel.

At Geneva Airport there was a wait of several hours for the Lufthansa flight to Innsbruck. This time Suzanna drove to Kitzbühel at a more sedate pace. She was peering intently through the windscreen, when I mentioned we could push up our speed — it was a fairly straight road.

"I don't like driving at night," was her reply. I noticed she was wearing glasses.

I sat back in the seat and thought about the conversation I had had earlier with Todd Stewart. The British Alpine Championships were coming up soon, and Todd wanted to know how fit I was after the collision with Suzanna, which had followed another incident on the slopes of Zauberberg Semmering.

It was not my fault on that occasion either. I had celebrated the New Year in Vienna with members of my mother's family. On New Year's Day a group of us decided to go skiing at Semmering, a family-friendly venue with pistes for beginners, pleasure skiers, snowboarders and freestyle skiers.

It also boasts the World Cup Panorama slopes, which can catch out the unwary, it certainly provides an adrenaline rush for the inexperienced.

In competition, you are straining every muscle to gain that extra burst of speed. Today, I was leisurely descending the Panorama enjoying the swish of the skis on the freshly powdered snow; the crisp air catching at my cheeks; that pleasurable feeling of being alone in a white wilderness.

Suddenly, a free-rider burst out the treeline, hurtled across the slope and careered straight into me. We tumbled over, rolling twenty or thirty metres down the hill before coming to rest in an untidy heap.

Fortunately, I was unhurt. The free-rider, who had been skiing off piste, appeared to be in a worse state. I called the medical centre on my mobile and shortly thereafter, paramedics and a stretcher party arrived on the scene.

As a precaution I was also taken to the centre, although shaken up and suffering bruising to my legs, after a brief examination I was released.

"So no lingering problems from the tumble in Semmering. That's good," remarked Todd. "And the effects of today's little incident should disappear before our home championships. Just don't over-exert yourself, Adam."

It was then I mentioned I was skiing the Streif.

"What! Even after Suzanna clattered into you? Phyllis told me you suffered severe bruising to the chest and shoulder."

He had stroked his chin. "Not at all wise, Adam. Suzanna is driving you back to Kitzbühel because you're not a hundred percent fit. In your state the Streif will make too many demands on you. It could put you out of the National Championships."

"I'll be OK. I'll take it easy during the first few days. I should be all right when it comes to qualifying." I tried to adopt a confident tone; but Todd knew as well as I that it would be touch and go. You have to be fit, really fit to accelerate on the steep sections, hold a tucked position over the jumps, and navigate the tight bends. The body takes quite a battering on the slopes of Mount Hahnenkamm.

"Well, you make sure you come back in one piece," was his parting remark.

What I did not mention to Todd was what followed the Semmering collision. But then there was no need for him to know. I had gone to check how the other skier was faring, and found him fully conscious sitting in a comfortable chair.

"Ah. . .you have very sharp elbows, Mein Herr," he said in German, grinning at me.

"And you are like an express train on skis, my friend."

"You're right." A brief grin, then his features took on a more serious cast. "It was entirely my fault. I hope you are not badly damaged. I did not expect anyone to be on the Panorama slopes this late in the day. There's a gap through the trees. I took it too quickly and came out at the wrong moment."

23

"No real harm done, to either of us hopefully. Let`s leave it at that."

"Thank you, you are most gracious. Perhaps, you would be kind enough to tell me your name."

"Adam Livesey. . .and you are?"

"Alexei Sokolov. You can probably tell I`m Russian. Whenever possible I come to Zauberberg Semmering, it suits my kind of skiing."

"Do you collide with many people on your trips to Semmering?"

He grinned. "You`re the first. . .though there have been a few near misses, especially, when skiing under the lights at night. Tell me, are you staying near here, or in Vienna?"

"Actually, I`m staying with my family in Vienna."

"Mm. . .are you free this evening? Perhaps I could buy you dinner, by way of atonement."

"I`d enjoy that. Where do you suggest?"

"What about the Gasthaus Stern on Braunhubergasse. Shall we say eight o`clock?"

I had been the first to arrive.

In fact, Sokolov did not appear for a further twenty minutes.

By that time, I was contemplating whether it might have been a hoax, or I had got the time wrong. When I looked up he was threading his way through the restaurant to our table: again his apologies were profuse.

"Adam, I`m so sorry, my boss wanted to discuss a problem, and I am told it`s down to me to solve. . .and quickly. Anyway, enough of that. Do you ski a lot?"

"Whenever I can, Alexei, which is most days during

the season."

"The season. . .are you a professional skier? No wonder you were on the Panorama. Livesey. . .I'm sure I've heard that name before. It will come to me. So, let's have a drink before we order, what would you like."

"A glass of white wine would be welcome."

Alexei called over the sommelier and requested a decent bottle of Sauvignon Blanc. That was soon emptied, and he called for another. By the time we had finished the first course, a third bottle had appeared.

"So tell me, Alexei, what do you do for a living," I asked, now feeling the mild effects of the wine.

"What do I do. . . good question. I can't tell you, Adam, other than to say I am the gopher for a man in high places."

He paused and mopped his brow with the napkin. Then topped up his glass. I demurred when he lifted the bottle in my direction.

Sokolov drank deeply while eating the main course. His words were becoming slurred when he began probing about the life I led as a skier. How I lived in a succession of hotel rooms; how my relationship worked with my coach and my agent. He appeared genuinely interested, even questioning me about the work I did commentating on winter sports.

"It seems you enjoy life, Adam. I thought I did. I was hoping to spend a few more days here, but now I find I have to leave early tomorrow morning."

He stared introspectively into his glass. Then beckoned the sommelier again.

"My friend and I would like a decent brandy."

Minutes later Sokolov made a brave attempt to drown the demands made upon him by his unknown employer.

"Here, have mine, Alexei. I`ll stick to the remnants of the wine."

I pushed the glass across the table.

"That`s civil of you, Adam. . .thank you. Do you know I`ve got a delightful apartment in Moscow, a car, a generous expense account."

He emptied the glass in one swallow, then leaned towards me. I got the full impact of alcohol fumes.

"But, do you know, I almost gave all that up. The man has no regard for his advisers."

It was obvious Alexei Sokolov was becoming maudlin. His speech was increasingly slurred, I missed some of what he said. In the event I paid the bill, and half-carried him to the entrance.

"He has no thought for others. . .that they may have a life as well. Do this, Alexei, do that Alexei."

By this time, I was holding Sokolov upright as the cool air of a winter`s evening heightened the result of him drinking too heavily.

"What do I care! He can stuff the job!" Alexei declared swaying sideways.

A taxi drew up and I helped him open the door.

He leaned on the taxi roof. "And I`ll tell him to his face. I`ll say, do your own dirty work. You may be at the top of the pile, but you should command by being respectful, and considerate. Stick your job, I`m leaving."

With that he fell into the taxi and I slammed the door shut.

Walking away it dawned on me that the man who had careered into me must be the personal aide to someone important in Russia.

CHAPTER FIVE

In January each year the ski world gets Hahnenkamm fever. Ski athletes from around the world gather in Kitzbühel to tackle The Streif, considered the world's most spectacular downhill run.

Everything is experienced by the competitors. Jumps of eighty metres; slopes with a sixty-five percent gradient; speeds of a hundred and forty kilometres per hour. The Hahnenkamm race requires a no-fear approach as it plunges off the mountain towards the town. Most competitors cross the finishing line in about two minutes — that is, if they finish the course. Just making it to the bottom is a feat in itself, and many racers' seasons have been ended on the treacherous descent.

For Kitzbühel, the Hahnenkamm event is the sporting and social highlight of the calendar. The build-up starts days before the event. The town is bursting at the seams, and partying goes on every night. Television pictures of wintry Kitzbühel circle the globe.

Suzanna drove into the Hotel Schweizerhof car park, and at reception I asked for a room for her.

"I am sorry, Herr Livesey, but the hotel is full. We have no spare rooms," the receptionist explained.

"Surely, you have a small room available for unexpected guests?" I asked.

She shook her head.

"What about other neighbouring hotels? Don't you have some form of arrangement with them?"

"I'm so sorry, Herr Livesey, everywhere is completely full. It's the Streif, you see. People are even sleeping in their cars."

"Don't worry, Adam. I'll share your room," declared Suzanna.

With that she picked up the key cards and headed for the lift.

When I awoke the next morning it took me a moment to recall where I was, and with whom. At that moment the bathroom door opened and Suzanna appeared wearing nothing more than a large towel.

"Right, I need to get dressed, so you can either take a shower, or turn your head to the wall."

I chose the latter, turning on my unbattered side.

It had been a novel experience sleeping with Suzanna. I had changed into pyjamas in the bathroom, when I came back into the bedroom, she had gathered all the cushions from the furniture and created a division down the middle of the Super King size bed.

She would have been perfectly safe. I could not have attempted anything strenuous in my present damaged state.

"Josh, may I introduce Suzanna Bancroft. She is our Super G skier in the British team. She came back with me to see how one prepares for the build-up to the Downhill."

Even to me it sounded a pretty thin reason for her being in Kitzbühel.

"Delighted to meet you, Suzanna," he said, shaking her hand. "Are you staying here or at another hotel?"

She didn't bat an eyelid.

"I couldn't get a room anywhere, Josh, so I'm bunking in with Adam."

Josh Finden nodded. "By the way Adam, I'm going out on the course with Jurgen and Maurice this afternoon, would you care to join us?"

I did not want to aggravate my bruised muscles, and declined the invitation.

"I don't know it at all, Mr Finden, would you mind if I joined you?"

"I'd be delighted, Suzanna. . .and call me Josh, everyone does. If you haven't got your gear, I can kit you out with everything you need. Come up to my suite. If there's nothing there, there's bound to be equipment in the prep room in the basement. Shall we say two o'clock at the ski lift?"

After an early lunch, to allow Suzanna to change in my — our — room, I sat in the bar with a glass of wine, then made my way over to the station, where Josh and his protégés were waiting.

Suzanna arrived wearing a purple and white padded catsuit beneath an open anorak and carrying her skis. Her blonde hair was tucked in a colourful bobble hat.

I could not help noticing she had a very appealing figure, and moved with the casual grace of an athlete.

Josh smiled a welcome.

"We'll show you, Suzanna, what skiers face doing the Streif. We'll halt by the Mouse Trap, or `Mausfalle` as they say in Austria. From the gate there is a steep slope, and that's where it gets interesting. The hill suddenly drops away and you fly for up to eighty metres. This is the steepest part of the hill and you're in the air approaching the Karussell, a tight right hander."

I said. "Don't forget, Josh, Suzanna is a Super G skier, she won't be too daunted by the Streif."

I left them to board the ski lift and made my way back to the Schweizerhof. In the hotel room I eased myself onto the bed and promptly fell fast asleep.

It was dark when Suzanna burst into the room, fell onto the bed and switched on a bedside light, waking me up.

"What time is it?" I asked, yawning.

"Nearly five o'clock. Come on sleepy head, join us downstairs."

I still felt only half awake when I met up with Josh, Jurgen and Maurice. Josh was still talking about the course when I took a seat beside Suzanna.

". . .could see it startled you. When you looked back up the slope, you murmured. `My God, if you're coming straight down, what speed would you doing?`"

"Well," Josh glanced in my direction, "ask him, he's skied the race several times."

I nodded. "About eighty miles an hour. So the line is critical when you are approaching any of the twists and turns."

"Well, I thought what I do, the Super G, was demanding enough," Suzanna said with feeling, "and that's off the lower slopes of a downhill course. Up there even the view at the start is frightening. As you say, Josh, the mountain literally falls away from your feet." She looked in my direction. "Rather you than me, Adam!"

Back in the room I eased myself again onto the bed.

The bathroom door opened and Suzanna marched in.

"Right, strip off," she announced. "I went to the pharmacy earlier, and bought a whole raft of ointments and creams to apply to your bruises."

"That's OK, I'll rub them on when I take a shower."

"God, you're such a prude," she said in an exasperated tone. "Are you worried you'll be defenceless and I'll ravish you?"

"Let's say I'm not used to strange women telling me to take my clothes off."

"So I'm a strange woman, am I?" Suzanna's face flushed in anger.

"Look, I didn't mean it quite like that," I mumbled. "What I meant was I didn't want to put you to any trouble."

"It's you who's in trouble. I want to know what you meant by strange... well?"

She was peering down at me as I lay on the bed.

I looked deep into her eyes. For several seconds I could not avert my gaze.

"Well?"

This time the emphasis was not nearly so strident.

"You're right, I was being a bit straight-laced. It was kind of you to consider how I might be feeling."

Suzanna nodded, then began emptying the bag from the pharmacy onto the bedside table. I eased myself up and slowly removed all but my underpants.

She went into the bathroom and returned with a large towel, which she spread on my side of the bed.

"OK, hop onto that." Suzanna pointed at the towel with a finger. "Mm. . ." she murmured, examining my chest. "That looks painful." She picked up a container and peered intently at the label. "Right, let's try this."

She squeezed a quantity of white cream into her hand and applied it to the area around my rib cage.

"Jesus!" I exclaimed, "that's bloody cold!"

"Don't be such a wimp," she chided. "Lie still while I rub it in."

I had to admit after twenty minutes, when Suzanna had finished coating my chest and shoulder, I felt much easier. It was less of a discomfort when I got to my feet.

"Thank you, nurse, that really feels much better. Though it smells a little, can I see the tube?"

"This is it." She passed the box and tube to me. "It's in Russian. However, the pharmacist recommended it."

"That's OK. Mm. . .it contains snake venom, I suppose that's what gives it the smell."

"Never mind that, you can't have a shower until later. I don't want you to wash off all my hard work," she declared. "Lie there, and let it soak in."

I must have fallen asleep.

I awoke with a start when Suzanna came out the bathroom. This time she was wearing a towelling robe.

She sniffed the air. "You're right, the smell is strong. Never mind it must be doing you good. You've been asleep for well over an hour. In fact, use the bathroom to shave while I dress. Remember, no showering."

As I was shutting the door, Suzanna said. "We are meeting Josh and others for dinner, so don't be too long."

Never before had I been told so often what to do. There have been a number of women in my life, but leading a bachelor existence I make my own decisions. One girlfriend had attempted to rule my life and had quickly become an ex-girlfriend. As I stared in the mirror and rubbed my chin, the slight stubble did not need removing. If Suzanna continues to tell me what to do, I'll be glad to see the back of her.

In the lobby we met Josh and several other skiers he managed. He had made a reservation at the Lois Stern restaurant, a short walk from the hotel.

At the table I found myself sitting between Josh and a fellow called Greg Nichols, also a Canadian. Chatting to him I learnt that he had just started making his way as a downhiller.

Suzanna was opposite talking animatedly to a fellow called Lars Oestensson, who had joined our table. Apparently, he was a member of the

Norwegian Nordic team, and his speciality was the Biathlon. To my mind making an undignified ascent of hills then skiing across the countryside for fifteen kilometres, interspersed with shooting at distant targets, was a ridiculous sport.

Moreover, every time I looked in her direction she was engaged in lively conversation. By the main course she gave him her mobile number. Oestensson must have been extremely amusing, for her laughter resounded round the table.

Josh touched my arm. "What's that you're eating, Adam? Whatever it is, it has an odd smell."

It must have been the cream Suzanna applied on me.

"Yes, I thought that too, Josh," I exclaimed. "It must be a herb the chef uses."

"Do you want me to call the waiter over, and get it changed?"

I glanced at Suzanna, who was grinning across the table at me.

"No, there's no need. The dish is enjoyable."

Two hours later we returned to the hotel.

"Who's for a nightcap?" asked Oestensson, looking directly at Suzanna.

"Good idea," she said gaily.

By this time the deadening effects of whatever Suzanna had used had evaporated, and my body was aching.

"I'm off to bed," I exclaimed, and headed for the lift. I was joined by Josh.

"I'd watch out, Adam," Josh said softly. "Lars is a

fast worker."

I pretended to be asleep when Suzanna came into the room.

I had arranged the cushions to divide the bed, and I lay there, eyes tightly shut, listening to her undress, use the bathroom, slip under the duvet and turn off the bedside light.

"Do you want me to apply any more cream?" Suzanna whispered. "I know you're not asleep."

"Yes I am," I said irritably.

"Is the discomfort of the bruises making you ratty?"

"I'm not ratty, just tired. Now go to sleep."

"Not when you're in a mood."

"Listen, I've got a tough day coming up tomorrow, and you aren't helping by wanting to have an argument," I said with some asperity.

"My. . .someone is in a bad humour. Was it because I went for a drink and didn't fulfil my role as your nurse?"

"Oh, go to sleep!"

Suddenly her bedside light came on, and Suzanna sat up in bed.

"God, you really are a pathetic creature. A few bruises and you want round-the-clock sympathy! Man up, Adam!"

I too sat up and turned on my light.

"As you were responsible for most of the bruises. . . you might at least feel some concern for what you did."

My voice trailed away as I glimpsed the teasing outline of her figure under the diaphanous material of the shift she was wearing.

35

"What do you think I'm doing here?" she exclaimed angrily, "when I could be in Tignes in the company of people I enjoy! That's it, I'm leaving first thing in the morning!"

She turned away from me and snapped off the light.

After a few minutes I broke the silence in a voice I hardly recognised.

"I would rather you didn't."

"Didn't what?" she muttered under the duvet.

"Leave."

"You can't apply the embrocation yourself, is that it?"

"You know it's not that."

The light came on again, and Suzanna sat up in an even more revealing posture. "So what do I know?"

I stared into her eyes. "That I like you being here. . .with me."

"And not with anybody else." She smiled, "Were you put out this evening because I was chatting with Lars. Is that why you went off to bed?"

"Perhaps." I smiled too.

She leaned forward, kissed me on the cheek and said. "Go to sleep, as you say, you've got a busy day ahead of you."

CHAPTER SIX

The course was now reserved for downhillers only. It would be closed to members of the public until race day was over on Sunday.

Today was the first training session; most competitors tended to ski the course marginally below their top speed, seeing it more as a run to lay down a marker. Flat out would be reserved for day two of training.

After breakfast, Suzanna rubbed my body and shoulder with several of the items she had bought. She then whispered. "Make sure you reach the bottom undamaged. The pharmacist sold me virtually all he had in stock."

I caught up with Josh Finden in a workshop close to the hotel.

"Adam, all set? I believe yours are over there. Ron has given them the once over." He nodded towards a rack holding pairs of skis, adding, "You OK? . . .you look a bit stiff."

"It's nothing, Josh. I slept a little awkwardly."

"Right. Let me know what the snow is like so I can pass it on to the others. By the way, you'll probably see Greg Nichols up at the start, he has just taken a gondola to the summit."

"It`s none of my business, Josh, but Greg appears older than the skiers you normally take on your books. Is this a change of policy?"

"Not really. Well slightly, perhaps. . .the thing is, he's fixed on the idea that the downhillers are more glamorous, carry more prestige, and earn more money. He paid heavily to join my band of trainers. Apparently, his family is not short of money and he has an indulgent father. Who am I to argue with double the normal fee?"

Competitors were gathering in a tent-like reception unit before making their way to the starting hut. Today, my skiing down the Streif would be adequate, nothing remarkable. It was not about setting a fast time, more to test my body. To discover if I could push myself on the second run tomorrow, to secure a place among the top thirty skiers going forward for the actual race on Saturday.

I walked over to Greg who was watching other skiers commence their first run. I stood beside him, and he murmured, "They don`t hang about, do they. Jeez, look at them go!"

"First time skiing the Streif, Greg?"

He turned his head slowly towards me and nodded.

"There aren`t many other courses that start as fast, with the exception of St. Moritz, but you`ll get used to it."

I snapped shut the bindings, put on my helmet and

gloves, and waited to be called forward. Now it was my turn. I leapt off the level area by the starting gate and quickly picked up speed on the run to Mausfalle.

I assumed a reasonable tuck position, and gasped at the strain on my chest and stomach muscles. Increasing speed, as I approached the Mausfalle, something was not right. I was slipping and sliding as I took the jump and tried to keep it flat and low. The right turn was difficult and I did my best to slow just to make it. It was halfway down before the skis performed better in the wetter snow. I cursed my luck while I waited for the result. It was posted — twenty-eighth place.

Josh came over. "I expected more from you than that!" he exclaimed. "What went wrong?"

"You tell me! Was a hard wax applied to my skis? I could hardly control them until I hit the Brückenschuss, the gliding flats."

"Of course!"

"Are you sure?"

I turned one of the skis over. Not immediately noticeable were tiny, reddish patches.

"Hard wax for icy conditions shows traces that are more blue to green. No sign of that. I could have had real problems at the top of the hill, Josh. That was bloody dangerous, I could have easily been amongst those who didn't make it to the bottom!"

"Or worse," he muttered.

"Weren't they checked?" I asked angrily.

"Well, I had others in the Downhill, so no. . .I'm sorry."

I waited for Greg to appear after three other skiers had finished the course.

When he came to a stop in the runout, he was breathless and excited.

"Man, that was really something," he grinned, panting heavily.

I felt as though I had been in a car accident.

"If we don't meet up again before tomorrow, let me wish you luck in qualifying."

Back in the hotel I closed the curtains and lay on the bed. I was not too unhappy with this morning's run, but it had taken a great deal out of me.

Suddenly, the door burst open and Suzanna marched into the room. She pulled back the curtains, leaned over me and studied my face.

"You look awful," she exclaimed. "Did you complete the course? Did you stay upright? Have you hurt yourself?"

"Yes, yes and no. But now I know what being kicked by a horse feels like."

"I've been speaking to Josh. He's expecting us to have lunch with him. Are you up to it?"

"Only if you can rub something into my protesting muscles."

"There's that smell again, I wonder what it is?"

We were in the hotel coffee shop eating a light snack.

"Actually, it could well be the embrocation I've begun using," I volunteered. "It works well, but has an unpleasant odour. It's OK when I'm in the open air."

"Oh, that's what it is," Josh remarked, and returned to quizzing me about the conditions on the course, and how Greg Nichols had performed.

"By the way, I was up by the Zielsprung. I watched you do that high speed jump this morning, and you looked a little untidy. You were not in a good tuck position, and coming into the finish that will lose you time when every fraction of a second is vital."

I looked resignedly to Suzanna.

"You're right, I could do better over that jump. I'll be ready for it tomorrow. This afternoon I'll work out in the hotel gym."

In the event a half an hour in the hotel sauna and a further session of Suzanna's healing hands, materially improved my movements in readiness for tomorrow's second training session.

CHAPTER SEVEN

The day dawned under a faultless, blue sky. The temperature was close to zero, and the air crisp but pleasant. I had struggled into my ski suit, and, with Suzanna`s help, managed to avoid too much twisting and pulling.

At the summit I joined the other racers waiting to be called forward. There was a tense, deferential silence, each of us mentally reviewing the course, and how best to ski it.

I was ready for a fast run.

I went through my routine of checking the ski bindings, breathing heavily into the goggles to demist them, donning helmet and gloves, adjusting the goggles, making sure they were secure.

I felt a frisson of excitement, a tightening of the stomach muscles, and a nervous shiver when I took my place behind the starting wand.

The countdown started, I waited for the starter`s hand to drop, then I pitched forward and was off down the slope, the prelude to the Mausfalle.

One minute, fifty-four point four four seconds later, having traversed the hill, fought to navigate the bends, and launched myself in death-defying leaps at the beginning and the end of the run, I came to a slithering halt.

Suzanna was there at the barrier around the runout to greet me.

I was in pain, really deep pain that wracked my body. For a while I was unable to stand erect. Eventually, more with her help, we made it back to the hotel and both used the sauna.

I stayed in there for almost an hour.

In our room Suzanna again applied the ointments and creams. I knew I smelt awful, but it brought some degree of comfort. While her hands rubbed my body, I fell fast asleep with the comforting thought I had made the top thirty in Saturday's race by finishing in eighteenth place.

CHAPTER EIGHT

Alexei Sokolov was seated at a breakfast table quietly congratulating himself. He had just pulled of a complicated plan which had brought the President and his mistress to Cape Idokopas.

Yesterday morning Tupolev had taken an Mi-38 helicopter to Smolensk — four hundred kilometres to the west. During the flight he had been heavily disguised, and when it touched down, was bundled into a Sukhoi SBJ private jet.

Meanwhile, Olga Petrova boarded a train to Kaluga, two hundred kilometres southwest of Moscow. A taxi took her to the VIP terminal at the nearby airport. When the jet landed, Petrova was whisked aboard, and the plane resumed its flight to Gelendzhik. A limousine with darkened windows had met the flight and delivered them to the Residence.

Sokolov was downing his third mug of coffee when he heard his name called. There was an angry tone to the shouting, which got progressively louder. It was the unmistakable voice of his master, Leoni Tupolev.

He mounted the stairs wondering what the

President would be demanding this time.

"Sokolov, come in here."

He was in the man's bedchamber, with Petrova seemingly asleep on a mountain of pillows.

"Don't look at her, look at this!" demanded Tupolev, and he dragged Sokolov to a side window.

"See that! I'm not going to have anyone overlook me, do you hear?"

Sokolov peered through the window.

On an adjacent promontory it was evident that very soon a substantial building would be erected, one that could well rival the splendour of the Residence. Not only that, it would also intrude upon Tupolev's panoramic view of the Black Sea.

"I want that, that monstrosity, erased, demolished, destroyed! No one is going to upstage me, spoil my simple pleasures! Don't just stand there. . .see to it immediately!"

A few hours later Sokolov's car came up to the electronically-controlled gates. Two guards came to the driver's window, checked the chauffeur, then with exaggerated caution, asked them both to step out the vehicle while they searched for any offensive weapons or bomb-making equipment.

Satisfied, the gates were opened and the car rolled to a standstill in the forecourt. Alexei jumped out and hurried through to the recreation area. Once again, Olga Petrova was asleep on a lounger while Tupolev swam, with slow strokes, up and down the olympic-size pool.

Eventually, when the required number of lengths

were completed, Tupolev climbed out the water and slipped on a towelling robe.

He dropped onto a lounger and looked up at his aide.

"Well? Have you stopped the building? When are they knocking it down?"

"Er. . .it may not be that simple," Sokolov said hesitantly. "All the contracts and documents are in order. The owner is fully authorised to build his mansion, and in that location."

"Then get the contracts, documents, whatever is necessary, torn up. I don`t pay you to sit on your arse and wring your hands. Get that site cleared, and do it now! Get hold of the owner and tell him to build somewhere else, not in my view!"

"I have discovered who the owner is, Leoni."

"I couldn`t care less. Just bloody-well tell him!"

"It`s Leonid Davidenko."

Tupolev stared hard at Sokolov.

"Yes," murmured the aide, "the head of the Bratva — Russia`s Mafia!"

CHAPTER NINE

It was Friday, a rest day, I slept until late morning. Eventually, I moved gingerly from the bed to the bathroom, showered, then changed into casual clothes and went in search of Suzanna.

She was in the hotel lounge talking to Lars Oestensson. It struck me again, this feeling she belonged to me, to no one else. After all she shares my bed, I felt irritated she sought his company.

"Hello, Adam," she turned and smiled in my direction. "I was telling Lars that next week I'm in Garmisch-Partenkirchen for a Super G, and would you believe, he is going to be there as well."

"Oh really."

Her eyes flashed. She was on the point of saying something biting when Josh and Greg came into the bar. Nevertheless, I received a cold stare before Josh suggested we all lunch in the hotel.

"What is it with you? I was just chatting to the guy, and found we had mutual commitments in Garmish."

We were in the bedroom.

"Really, Adam, act your age, you're like some adolescent schoolboy," she said, tossing her blonde hair in indignation.

She advanced towards me. "Let's get this straight, I'll spend time when and with whom I please. If you don't accept that, then first thing tomorrow morning it's back to Tignes."

She stood in front of me looking into my eyes.

I could not break from her gaze. Unthinking, I did what could well have been the end of a tempestuous friendship. I leaned forward put my arms around her, and kissed her.

I heard her gasp. Oh God, I thought fleetingly, that's it. I've overstepped the line. Then I felt the pressure of our lips increasing, and her arms encircling me.

When we broke away. I still held onto to her. I didn't want to see recrimination on her face. But, eventually, we parted.

Suzanna was smiling. There were no icy stares, no harsh words about being too forward. "My, do you kiss all the women you've only known a couple of days like that, Adam?" she exclaimed.

I blushed. "No, of course not."

Suzanna nodded. "No, I don't think you do. Perhaps I'm privileged."

She touched my lips with a finger. "So what shall we do this afternoon?"

"How about a walk through the town. A gentle stroll by the lake, perhaps?"

"Sounds good to me." Then a thought struck her. "Somewhere I saw an article in a magazine about dog sledding in Tignes. Can we find out more about it? I wouldn't mind trying that."

When I enquired of the concierge, he made a booking for the afternoon ride just for Suzanna. The constant jarring of travelling in a sled would not have been the sensible preparation for tomorrow's race.

I accompanied Suzanna to the number sixteen bus stop by lakeside where, according to the concierge, we would find the dogs and sleds. He had also advised that Suzanna wear her warmest clothes, stout boots and thick gloves.

When we arrived her sled and dogs were already waiting.

Apparently, the handler, or `musher`, as he was known, announced over the baying of the dogs, that he would be taking her around the lake. "So sit back and enjoy the scenery," he told her.

With a mere word from him they were off. A brief wave from Suzanna, and she was gone.

The ride was going to take about thirty minutes. Not enough time to walk into the town and back, so, for a while, I chatted to one of the handlers. He was clearly fond of the dogs, and took me over to where they were tethered. As we approached they began barking, not aggressively, more he explained, to be chosen to haul the next sled ride.

"They just love running in the snow," he explained. "The Husky, Samoyed and Malamute breeds are amazing physically. They love to haul a sled in the cold, and out in the wilderness they would run for hours."

Eventually, Suzanna's sled appeared, coming across the frozen lake. The handler, who was standing next to me, must have noticed my concern, for he remarked.

"Don`t worry, at this time of year we could drive a car across to the other side."

Suzanna eased herself out the sled and thanked the `musher` for such a remarkable experience. "You must try it, Adam. It`s fantastic. We`ll come again when you`ve fully recovered. Thank you, darling."

She stretched up and kissed me in a very inviting way.

All the way back to the Schweizerhof she rhapsodised about the sled ride while holding tightly on my arm.

The draw for starting places was scheduled to take place at six o`clock in the evening. I had recovered from my irritation with the wrong wax; and when we gathered to choose the race order, Josh was standing a few metres away. By way of a belated apology, I said. "The other day I was upset about the waxing, but these things can happen, I know that, Josh. I should not have behaved like an adolescent schoolboy." I smiled at the remark, for Suzanna had made that comment of me.

He nodded and shrugged. "Forget it, my boy. I hope you get a decent number."

I walked back to Suzanna.

"Well, did you apologise?" she murmured.

"Yes. . .I said I would," I added, sitting beside her.

Without thinking I reached out for her hand, and squeezed it gently. Puzzling in a way, I had never done that before in previous relationships. She seemed to read my thoughts.

"You`re not one to wear your feelings on your sleeve, are you?"

I thought about what she said. "No. . .no, I guess I`m not. At least I didn`t think I did. Until now. . ."

"Not like me," she mused. "I tend to do things without giving the consequences much thought. Like now."

She half rose from her seat, leaned forward, and kissed me in full view of the others.

"See what I mean?" she grinned, falling back into her chair.

The consequence of that act was me blushing the deepest red I had ever displayed. A good thing it was dark and no one could see my embarrassment.

***

Unlike some other skiing disciplines, the Super G and the Downhill are one-run-only events. Thus, the running order is all-important, for the course terrain and speed change the more racers ski its surface.

The ten top competitors choose their skiing bibs between the odd numbers, one and nineteen. The even numbered bibs, between two and twenty, are drawn by the next ten competitors. Racing bibs between twenty-one and thirty drawn by the last ten skiers. Fortunately, I was in the second category, but I only managed to draw twentieth placing.

When Suzanna closed the bathroom door, I sat on the bed and reviewed what had just happened. I kicked off my shoes and leaned against the bedhead. I could not believe my good fortune. One thing was certain . . .even though painful, I would not be applying any of the awful smelling cream to my body tonight.

I awoke with light filtering through the curtains.

I was still wearing my shirt and trousers.

An arm, not mine, was laying on my chest.

Then it dawned on me, I had drifted to sleep while Suzanna occupied the bathroom. Not the most gallant when her kiss had heralded more was to come. Particularly, as the arm signified there were no longer any cushions down the middle of the bed.

I moved slightly.

"So you are awake then," came a dreamy response.

I sat up when the arm was removed.

"Suzanna, I can explain..."

"Well, it had better be good. You were not only asleep when I came out the bathroom, you had a self-satisfied smile on your face."

"I guess the smile was one of quiet joy that I hadn't had my face slapped, or you hadn't called the hotel manager when I made advances." I said ruefully.

She sat up beside me. "Look, I knew you were tired. You had a demanding day on Thursday."

She leaned sideways and kissed my cheek.

I turned towards her and we kissed. Slowly, with a quiet passion I had never before experienced.

"Wow," Suzanna exclaimed. "That was no ordinary kiss...you really meant it," she murmured.

I moved towards her, and let out a gasp as pain once more wracked the right side of my body.

"Adam, no more sudden moves...more's the pity. Go and have a shower, and afterwards I'll apply some of the painkilling salves to help you through the day."

We had breakfast with the others.

This time Suzanna sat next to me, repeatedly touching my arm, passing items on the table to me with a smile, and glancing frequently in my direction.

Josh looked over, grinned, and raised a quizzical eyebrow.

To counter any remark, I asked him if the skis were with his technician.

"All ready for you, Adam. No problems this time. Edges sharpened and waxed. You're ready to go."

CHAPTER TEN

An Austrian won the Super G, which drove his home supporters into ecstasies of joy. The whole of Kitzbühel was a sea of national flags and good-humoured revelry.

Next was the Downhill: the race that draws the crowds, which most captures people`s imagination.

At number twenty, I joined other competitors in a gondola to the summit. The race was scheduled to start at one thirty, and many were sheltering in the reception tent sponsored by Red Bull.

Gradually, those before me were called into the starting hut, ready to take their place at the gate. When it was my turn, I shuffled forward, and watched the skiers in front of me descending the run in their minds, bodies twisting and turning as they rehearsed their flight down the course.

Perhaps it's because of the danger, or the possibility of glory, but as those around me prepared to propel themselves off the mountain, an eerie calm prevailed. I too went through the course in my mind. I believe everyone visualises the skiing line, for I was well aware the Streif doesn't forgive mistakes.

"Livesey, number twenty!"

I inched towards the start gate. There was a small crowd in the hut, several coaches and a number of race officials.

I placed my two ski poles over the wand and waited for the customary gap between skiers to count down.

I peered towards the precipice of the Mausefalle. My leg muscles tightened as I readied myself. Suddenly a radio crackled, the skier ahead of me had missed a gate and come off the course into the netting.

I stood back. Ten, then fifteen minutes passed. Calmness was starting to ebb away. More crackling radio. The marshal turned to me, `OK, alles ist klar`.

In a self-imposed haze I moved once more to the starting gate. Ski poles over wand, *beep-beep-beep-beep-beeeeep*, three pushes, six strides, and I was away, shouting "Go . . .Go. . .Go!"

A mere seven seconds later I was airborne over the Mausefalle at seventy miles an hour.

Landing I came immediately to the section of hairpin turns called the Karussell. Then an abrupt transition to a flatter, rutted terrain, followed by compression forces of more than three G's.

After the Karussell, the Steilhang, which really is as steep as hell, the pitch fell away my edges biting into the rock-hard snow. The slope dropped further into a pair of big swinging; adverse camber turns. This is the crux of the course; you have to nail the second turn and carry as much speed as possible into a long, relatively flat glide through the woods, the Brückenschuss.

I was coming up fast to the Seidlalm. A blind jump where the angle and lift-off point are difficult to gauge. To hit the right line, I aimed for the hospital I could see in Kitzbühel below.

Shivering prior to the race I was now sweating profusely in my thin skiing one piece. But what did I care. Exhilaration over-rode thoughts of personal safety as I threw myself down the hill.

After two kilometres my legs were on fire. The constant chuddering going into the turns; holding the tuck when flying was beginning to tell. But I would not submit to the Hahnenkamm mountain that easily.

A quick ninety degree turn and I'm confronted with the blind jump of the Hausberkante. I won't see the landing area until I'm airborne, when it's too late to adjust the trajectory. Then, a fraction of a second after landing, I hit the Traverse, a rough hillside of shimmering ice which pushes me hard right, in the direction of the netting fence. Surrendering to G-forces now would be catastrophic.

Coming out of the Hausberkante, the course is making more physical demands upon me. I'm short of breath and panting hard.

The Traverse flows into a striking right turn, and I'm accelerating up to ninety miles an hour, again into a compression which pushes me further into a deep tuck for the Zielschuss, the final jump.

I sail close to eighty metres, gradually losing height as my legs begin to droop through fatigue. Hitting the rutted surface My momentum carries me down the Rasmusleitn to the finish.

I had made it.

My head is bowed, I am exhausted.

"Adam, Adam, over here!"

Suzanna is ten metres away leaning over the barrier.

I struggle to her, and she wraps her arm tightly about me.

"That was wonderful, darling. Now take off that blasted helmet so I can kiss you!"

When we broke apart I asked. "What time did I do?" I had not checked the clock.

"One minute fifty-two point seven! Wow, you're in fifth place!" she cried. She hugged me again. "That's fantastic, to pull up so many places."

I stayed in fifth place, for all ten remaining skiers did not get close to my time.

We celebrated that night, but not before I had lain in a cold bath for nearly an hour. How athletes immerse themselves in ice is beyond me. Anyway, I had encountered enough ice on the Streif.

Suzanna's soothing hands and a good measure of her salves were applied, so that when we left the room, I was relatively upright.

Once again, Josh had booked a table at the nearby Stern restaurant. This time I was seated between Josh and Suzanna.

The wine flowed, conversation was light-hearted, the laughter carefree. I glanced across the table at Lars Oestensson, and raised my glass in his direction.

He lifted his glass towards me and smiled.

"Adam, you did well finishing fifth."

I tried to assess what was really behind that smile. `You've won the lady for the moment. . .but wait until we are together in Garmisch-Partenkirchen.`

Josh remarked. "You did well today, Adam, especially being in the twentieth spot. You must have had a rough ride."

I nodded thoughtfully. "It had its moments."

"So, let's discuss the next downhill. Are we sticking to the schedule? If so it's St. Moritz, and we're on the slopes in eight days' time."

"Is it safer than the Streif?" queried Suzanna.

"Most of the downhill course is," remarked Josh. "But there are a few elements you have to avoid, particularly the start."

Suzanna looked at me in an odd way, which I could not fathom out.

It was a splendid evening, and we had all eaten well, and perhaps drunk a little too much.

She had the bathroom first. I lay back on the bed thinking about Garmisch. I was not going to give Lars Oestensson the opportunity to be alone with Suzanna. He had been trying to steal her from me, so perhaps saluting him at dinner had been tinged with just a hint of one-upmanship.

Swathed in a robe Suzanna came into the bedroom.

"I'll drive you to the airport tomorrow," I said when she sat beside me. "What time is your plane from Innsbruck?"

"No need...I've already had the offer of a lift."

"Oh! Who made the offer?"

She turned towards me. "Lars did. He is driving over to Garmisch, and offered to drop me off at the airport. Pity I didn't bring my gear with me, I could have gone all the way."

"What do you mean by that?"

"Well..."

"That bloody Oestensson! Always trying to muscle in," I said, interrupting her. "He's not going to get away with it. And what do you mean `going all the way`?"

"All I meant was. . ."

"And another thing," I said hotly. "I'm coming to Garmisch! I'm not leaving you on your own with him."

"Oh, you don't trust me?" Suzanna replied, her face glowing red. "I can look after myself. I don't need you as a chaperone! Furthermore, you were playing one-upmanship at dinner tonight. Grow up, Adam!"

I stood up, and so did she. We faced one another.

"No I damned well wasn't!" I leaned forward. "Take that back! I don't like him, true enough, but I can be civil."

"Shan't! It was obvious to everyone what you were doing."

Our faces were almost touching, both of us angry and shouting.

I was about to let forth another tirade, but suddenly stopped short. Instead, I took her face in my hands and gently kissed her.

"I don't want to argue. . .least of all with you," I said in a low voice.

I kissed her again. This time more intently. I could not help myself. There was a sigh and Suzanna hungrily sought my lips.

We fell back together onto the bed.

Leaning over there was not a hint of pain when I stretched out and turned off all the lights. In the dark I began to make up for all the lost opportunities of sharing a bed with the woman I really cared for.

Later, Suzanna was lying across my chest when she whispered. "By the way, I turned down his offer."

"Now you tell me. Damn you, Bancroft," I said, nuzzling her ear. "I was put out at the thought of you and Lars travelling together. And worse, being in Garmisch with him."

She chuckled, "I was hoping you might feel up to converging before I went back to Tignes. That's why I applied much more than I normally rub on you. The trouble was you got cross with me. . .never mind, the combination worked."

"Combination?"

"Mm, the creams to ease your stiffness," she chuckled openly, "no, not that. . .your chest and shoulder. However, the extra dosage worked, as did arousing a little jealousy."

I laughed. "I didn't know you were that scheming. I shall have to watch for the warning signs in the future," I exclaimed, holding her even closer to me.

She sighed. "Now that's what I really call convergence, Mr Livesey."

That night I lay there thinking deeply about the young woman beside me. Was this the beginning of an enduring romance, or had circumstances created a fleeting desire for each other, only to evaporate once Suzanna returned to Tignes.

With a rush came the feeling I did not want to lose her. I would not let it come to nothing. Until now it had been light-hearted affection. As I saw it, I had twenty-four hours to turn it into something stronger.

***

"I tried, though I doubted it would have the desired effect. He is a professional. They often know in an instant if there's a problem, and ski accordingly."

"You told me, in the excitement of the race, he could well ignore faults with his skis until it was too late. There was every likelihood he would crash out at the top of the hill."

"True. . .but I was told it had to appear accidental. Such requirements introduce greater possibilities of survival. On this occasion that's what happened."

"Listen, we are running out of time. You have your orders. Make sure this mission is completed within the next few days, or you will not enjoy the leniency I am presently showing you. . .do you understand?"

CHAPTER ELEVEN

When my mobile rang there was no way I could disentangle the bare arms and legs to free myself before the caller hung up. I spent time moving various parts of our anatomies while Suzanna slept peacefully on.

In the bathroom I phoned the number belonging to Josh Finden.

"Didn`t see you at breakfast, my boy. Everything OK?"

I glanced at my watch. Ten fifteen.

"Sorry, Josh I overslept. It was quite demanding yesterday."

I did not mention that it was just as demanding last night.

"Well, I`ve spoken to others, and the consensus of thought is we meet this afternoon at four o`clock in the hotel lounge. Is that OK with you?"

"Sure, I`ll be there."

***

"Well? What have you to tell me? I hope, for your sake, it is news I want to hear, that the contract has been

fulfilled."

"Er, not quite. But it soon will be. His lady friend is going back to Tignes today. My bet is that he will accompany her to Innsbruck Airport. I know for a fact Livesey will be back here for a meeting in Kitzbühel this afternoon, which means he will be on the road, there and back, for two hundred kilometres. . .our opportunity to close out the problem."

"Don't phone me again until the task I'm paying you for is completed, do you hear?"

"Perfectly."

CHAPTER TWELVE

Suzanna hurriedly packed, but had a tussle trying to push her case onto the back seat. "It`s a pity it hasn`t got four doors. I usually travel with more than one case," she said in exasperation.

We made good time, and at the Wörgl junction turned onto the A12 autobahn heading west for Innsbruck.

I dropped Suzanna at the airport terminal with an hour to her flight. She kissed me, grabbed her case and said hurriedly, "See you in Garmisch at the Hotel Riessersee tomorrow night. Don`t forget, the Riessersee!"

As she disappeared through the entrance doors, a sense of loneliness enveloped me. I sat there for a moment collecting my thoughts, until someone in a uniform tapped on the window and pointed to the NO PARKING sign.

I wound down the window. "Can you tell me where the Hertz desk is?"

He gave me directions and I drove round to the hire company`s parking lot. Thereafter, I made my way through the terminal building and joined a short queue at the car hire desk.

There was a fellow about my age in front of me, and

he wanted a basic model, the same as I had had.

My exchange was quickly accomplished; particularly as I was paying more to upgrade to Volvo estate car. That should hold Suzanna's belongings I thought.

I rejoined the autobahn and began the return journey to Kitzbühel at a leisurely pace. I wanted to think deeply about the woman who was now commanding all my attention. I had never met a female so decisive, so unrestrained by convention, who knew what she wanted from life. I had been fond of a number the women during my twenty-eight years; and when we parted there had never been any rancour, no harsh words — most had remained good friends, though never life-partners.

I had drifted into the fast lane and blaring horns quickly brought me to my senses. I increased speed and brought the car back to the inside lane.

Concentrating more on the road, I glanced in the rear mirror and noticed a large Mercedes a hundred metres further back. It was also in the inner lane travelling at the same pace as myself. Clearly, the driver was in no hurry to join the headlong rush of vehicles as they flashed by.

My thoughts turned again to Suzanna. How committed were we to each other? Was it a romance that had blossomed too quickly to be nothing more than a brief infatuation? Out of sight for a few days, could it become out of mind? Like a candle that flares just before a puff of wind extinguishes the flame?

Driving slower than usual, I became aware how closely the autobahn followed the twists and turns of the River Inn. It seemed to meander under the roadway, first on the righthand side, then on the left.

I had driven about sixty kilometres, and passing a large lorry was approaching the turn-off to Jenbach.

When I glanced in the rear-view mirror, the large Mercedes had switched lanes and was accelerating fast. Its lights flashed, and I hurriedly swung back into the inside lane behind a small, blue, two-door Kia. The same as I had hired until exchanged for the Volvo.

I noticed that the slip road was closed for repair. A signboard indicated drivers should continue to the next junction then turn back to reach Jenbach from the opposite side of the autobahn.

The Mercedes flashed past me and drew level with the small car. Suddenly it swerved inwards. There was a loud thump and screeching of metal. The offside wing of the Kia in front of me disintegrated, the windscreen shattered into glass droplets.

I braked and swung onto that part of the carriageway leading to the slip road, and heard another earth-shaking bang when the Mercedes collided with the Kia`s rear end. It sent the car careering up the slip-road, through a red and white barrier, hitting a loose section of the low Armco fender it was tossed into the air to smash against a tree.

I could not believe my eyes; the Mercedes had not faltered but continued away from the accident at breakneck speed.

I came to a halt. Grabbing my mobile phone I dialled 133 for the police, and 144 for emergency rescue and ambulance. Several others, who had stopped behind me, got out their vehicles and followed me up the slip road.

The car had landed upside down and was a total wreck. I knelt on the ground and peered into the interior. The driver was hanging from the safety belt, his neck at a peculiar angle. There was no sign of life.

In a matter of minutes several police cars and an

emergency service vehicle appeared on the scene.

"Let me introduce myself. I am Officer Johannes Schmidt of the Bundespolizei. I shall ask you some questions, and, if it's OK with you, Herr Livesey, I shall record our conversation. Shall we go to my car?"

So they already knew my name. Then I realised I had given it when phoning for help. I felt a little wobbly as we made our way back down the slip road. No doubt the reaction to the crash.

When I ducked into the back seat, the officer placed a hand on my head.

He then opened the other rear door and climbed in beside me.

The policeman explained that the crash vehicle was a hire car, and they had been in touch with Hertz, informing them it was a total write-off and instructing them to make arrangements for the vehicle's removal. Then the interview became more personal.

"First of all, tell me, what were you doing on the autobahn?"

"I had just dropped someone off at Innsbruck Airport, and was making my way back to Kitzbühel."

"What are you doing in Kitzbühel? Holidaying or business? Can you tell me where you are staying?"

"At the Hotel Schweizerhof."

Schmidt looked at me strangely. "This week of the year the hotel is reserved mostly for skiers and those associated with skiing." He peered at me again. "Wait a minute...Livesey...didn't you come fifth in the Streif?"

I nodded.

The atmosphere changed in the car. "The way you

came out the Seidlalm," he shook his head. "Did you know where you were heading? That`s a blind jump, but there appeared to be no hesitation. How did you do that?"

"I fixed my path by aiming for the hospital in the town. You can see part of it quite plainly from the upside of the jump."

He had forgotten the recording, and was keen to talk about competition skiing. I had to remind him about my statement.

"Of course, Herr Livesey, of course."

I recounted details of the journey from when I left Suzanna at the airport.

"I stayed in the inside lane, drove at a modest speed, rarely went above eighty kilometres an hour. It was about half past two, I was close to Jenbach, when I noticed two things...the slip road to the town was closed; and a large Mercedes sped past me in the outside lane. When we came close to the turn-off there was a huge bang as the Mercedes drove into the car in front of me. In fact, it hit the Kia twice. The second impact pushed the car up the slip road, where it crashed through the barrier, hit the Armco rails, pitched over and came to rest against the tree."

"Was it an accidental collision, do you think?"

"If it had been once, I could have been persuaded it was accidental. But the Mercedes hit the Kia twice. What is more, the Mercedes didn`t stop!"

"Did you get its registration?"

"No, I`m sorry. I only recall it was black."

"Tell me," said Officer Schmidt. Was there any possibility the Kia pulled out and hit the Mercedes?"

"No chance. It was a flagrant attempt to run the Kia off the road," I replied vehemently.

There was a tap on the window. Schmidt lowered it a fraction to hear what one of his men had to say.

"Excuse me, Herr Livesey, I shall be back in a moment."

Ten minutes later, the door opened on my side. "Herr Livesey would you come with me, please?"

We walked over to a white BMW parked by the other police car.

A man in his forties was talking urgently to the policeman who had drawn Schmidt away. As we approached the car doors opened and the man's family got out.

"Herr Livesey sit in the front passenger seat, please." Schmidt said, and climbed into the rear with his colleague.

The owner took his seat behind the wheel, and turned on the ignition.

A small screen came to life, and without a word spoken, we watched a re-enactment of the incident captured on a dashcam.

The BMW was in the outside lane behind the Mercedes, and caught the moment it slammed into the hire car and sent it to destruction up the slip road. Schmidt asked if we could see it again. I realised why. The registration plate was indistinct, no one could decipher the number. What was evident was a black Mercedes hitting the Kia, and killing the driver.

Armed with the evidence, Schmidt contacted Hertz, and explained that it was a hit-and-run incident and the late driver had been blameless.

***

His cell phone rang.

"Well? Have you completed the assignment?"

"I believe so."

"What do you mean, `believe so`? Didn`t you check?"

"The car went through the barrier and crashed through trees. Whether it plummeted into the river was hard to tell. But there were emergency rescue vehicles police cars and heavy lifting equipment strewn all over the slip road. Later, from the Jenbach bridge, I managed to get a glimpse of the car when it was lifted onto the roadway. It was a shattered wreck. No one could have survived that and lived."

"Good! You have done well. I shall make the agreed transfer."

CHAPTER THIRTEEN

"You've changed the car?" Suzanna's gaze turned to me. "And why are you limping? You were all right when I left you twenty-four hours ago. What have you been up to, Adam?" she asked in a resigned tone.

She had been waiting in the lounge of the Hotel Riessersee, and seen me arrive. We took the lift and walked along the corridor to her room in silence.

Opening the door, she pushed me through and slammed it shut.

"OK, out with it!"

I took a deep breath. "After I dropped you at the airport, driving back to Kitzbühel someone ran the car in front of me off the road. I ricked my ankle when I ran to help the driver."

Her eyebrows twitched. "Why would anyone do that? Are you sure you weren't too tired to be a reliable witness??" She smiled at the thought. "After all, we did spend rather a hectic night together."

"The police examined the evidence and declared it was not accidental, but deliberate. According to an eyewitness, his dashcam clearly showed a Mercedes careering into a small blue Kia. When I got to the car it was a total wreck, and the driver is dead."

"My god! What did the driver of the Mercedes say?"

"He didn`t, he just carried on driving."

"The Mercedes didn`t stop! Did anyone get its registration? Oh, you poor thing, that must have been harrowing for you." She enveloped me in her arms, and held me tight. "Oh, my poor darling. Fancy having to witness that. Lay on the bed and rest for a while," Suzanna insisted. "I sincerely hope the police catch whoever did it. Do you feel up to going down to dinner, or shall we have room service?"

"No, let`s eat downstairs," I replied. "Who is here from the team?"

Pulling the duvet over me, Suzanna answered. "Well, there`s Todd, of course, our beloved performance director, Angela, Lisa and Jeff in the slalom, Mike Roberts and I in the Super Gs, and Johnny Biggs, giant slalom. Seven of us."

We lay close on the bed.

An hour passed and Suzanna stirred beside me. "I`ll have a quick shower, and let you have the bathroom afterwards. I`m bound to take longer than you."

"Tell me," I murmured, "have you mentioned to any of them that we are sharing your room? How do we appear? Together, or shall I come to the table a few minutes after you?"

She thought for a moment, then replied. "I`ll mention it casually over breakfast, when their minds are more on their respective competitions. So leave your arrival at the dinner table a little while after me."

I allowed a good twenty minutes before I entered the dining room and made my way through the throng of diners. They were all busy chatting and did not witness my approach.

"Look, it's Adam," Suzanna exclaimed. She jumped up and sat me on a chair beside her.

"Adam, how welcome you are!" declared Todd. "Have you come to give us moral support?"

"He would have done better if his skis were in shape in the qualifying run," blurted out Suzanna. "Someone applied the wrong wax, and. . ."

She stopped and reddened slightly.

"Of course, Suzanna, you were there to cheer him on," Todd grinned. "No after-effects from the Streif I hope, bearing in mind you're competing at St. Moritz next week?"

"No, I'll be fine. One or two aches and pains, but nothing to stop me competing in the downhill."

I could feel Suzanna's eyes on me. Willing me to say I'm pulling out of the run. I suddenly noticed Greg Nichols at the far end of the table. He smiled and waved an arm.

"Are you skiing this week, Greg? What have you entered?" I asked.

Todd answered for him. "Greg's like you Adam. He's here as an idle spectator. Though, I suppose you'll be rooting for Suzanna in the Super G."

He grinned knowingly. Suzanna went a shade redder, and I studied the menu more intently.

"They all know? How could they?"

"At first, I didn't have a clue. However, halfway through the evening I went to the ladies' room. When I was fixing my make-up Lisa walked in, she's skiing the slalom. As she headed for a cubicle she said over her shoulder, 'I didn't know you and Adam were an item. Still, I approve your choice, Suzanna.'"

"I waited until she was checking herself in the mirror, and said casually, `What do you mean an item? We are friends, that`s all."

"Then she said, not according to Greg. He told us you shared a room in Kitzbühel, and I understand Adam`s staying in your room here in Garmisch. You know how we all love a little gossip. . .juicy tidbits of news spread like wildfire, especially when it involves team members."

"I didn`t think of Greg Nichols," I murmured. "As you know, he`s one of Josh`s protégés. I didn`t realise he knew Todd, or I would have been a little more distant when you and I were together."

"Well, it`s out now," Suzanna said, carefully putting out her arms to hold me carefully. "So we can go down for breakfast together," she said kissing me gently.

At heart, I tend to be a shy person. Suzanna, on the other hand, was quite blasé, and took my hand as we walked towards the team table. But nothing was said, no knowing glances, no raised eyebrows.

"Don`t forget, girls," declared Todd, "we shall take to the hills at eleven to see what the snow`s like. Then we`ll check out the slalom course, and afterwards, the Super G run, Suzanna. After lunch, we`ll reverse the order for the men. First the Super G with Mike, then the slalom with Johnny. Are you skiing with us, Adam?"

I caught a glance from Suzanna before I answered.

"Perhaps, later, Todd. I`ve got to speak with Josh Finden."

Greg Nichols ambled over. "We are out on the runs

this morning, checking out the slalom and Super G courses, Greg," Todd explained. "Care to join us?"

"Great. . .I'll borrow some kit from the hotel."

"Don't forget, Greg," Todd commented. "You have to keep well to one side to assess the layout of the slalom, and we can only check the Super G from a distance. The first time you get a close-up of the actual run is on race day."

"No trespassing then, just a visual check?"

"That's right."

"No problems, Todd. I'll catch up with you shortly."

I was told to rest on the bed after my exertions skiing the Streif, and Suzanna would check lunchtime, to make sure. In fact, that suited me. The accident at the slip road had shaken me more than I realised.

I retreated under the duvet, and was soundly asleep, unaware of her presence when she returned to the room. So much so, I missed lunch and it was mid-afternoon when I eventually surfaced.

Suzanna woke me and told me of her day. Recounting aspects of the course to be wary of, the current snow quality, and who, of the big names, were competing.

"Are you up to assessing the run with me tomorrow morning," Suzanna ventured. "I have an hour and a half to inspect the positions of the gates when they are set up. Your comments would be useful."

"Of course. What time does the assessment begin?"

"Ten thirty. The race takes place at twelve," murmured Suzanna.

"Fine. I can never remember how many gates there are. What's the number?"

"Thirty. And you can`t ski the course until the actually race."

"So you have to ski as fast as you can, yet not miss a gate? Must be hard on the knees."

"What`s wrong with my knees?"

"From what I`ve seen . . .they`re absolutely perfect," I grinned. "Like the rest of you."

"Mmm. . .I think I shall order some tea. There`s nothing like it. . . when it`s with a little sympathy."

We had dinner in the room that evening, and refrained from any form of exertion when we went to bed. Suzanna had to be fresh in mind and body, not tired or distracted.

So until she went to sleep I chastely held her hand.

Tomorrow would be a big day for her. To my mind, her place in the British team was secure; but she was adamant she had to finish in the top ten to be sure. Physically, Suzanna was tall for a woman, and was well-proportioned with strength in her legs and upper body. Ideal for the demands of Super G.

Super G, or to give its full title, Super Giant Slalom, is a combination of a shortened version of downhill and the stretched principles of slalom. Even though the distances between the gates are far greater, you need speed and agility to be successful. Moreover, you only get one shot at negotiating the run. Top Super G skiers have good memories. They picture the course in their mind solely from the brief exposure ninety minutes before hurtling down the slope to the finishing line.

And then it was Suzanna`s turn.

At first, I thought she was too fast to make the first gate, but she accomplished the turn with ease. Quickly lining up the second, she was already sizing up the third. My heart leapt at every gate. I was not aware of twisting my body in tune with hers. The heart-stopping moments when she corrected her balance with a slight drag of a pole; when she briefly drifted outside the blue course lines, when she scrapped past a flagged gate marker.

When she crossed the line I was shouting at the top of my voice.

Third! With just several skiers to come. I couldn't believe it. Suzanna had been so impressive. I stood behind the barrier cheering. Off came the skis, she leaned over the boarding and kissed me. I stared into her face, and murmured, "Remarkable!"

In the event, one of the final skiers pushed her into fourth place by six hundredths of a second. But it did not matter. Her performance had been outstanding.

Suzanna was happy. She said breathlessly. "In future I want you always in the crowd when I'm competing."

"That's where I want to be!" I added. At that moment I felt something deeper, more meaningful, had come into our burgeoning relationship.

At the dinner table that evening Todd recounted how I had lived every twist and turn of Suzanna's run in the Super G.

"I was standing next to him," he said smiling. "Would you believe he was crouching at the start, and pushed off when she did. I moved out the way as I watched his performance. Leaning one way, then the other. Arms waving, legs stamping."

He imitated my movements, much to the merriment of the team. Suzanna smiled, and rubbed my shoulder. She remarked, "If it's that which places me in the top ten, I'm all for it!"

"You're right," said Todd, "with a few pom-poms, Adam, could become our official cheerleader. Just don't stand too close to him."

The next two days seemed to fly by. Despite Todd's nomination of me as cheerleader, other members of the team did not fare as well as Suzanna. Intriguingly, I wanted to be with her every waking moment, as well as every sleeping one.

But the time came when the team were returning to Tignes to prepare for the competition in St. Moritz, I had stowed my gear in the minibus along with the others. Suzanna was about to board, when uncaring of every watchful eye, I hugged and kissed her.

Of course I would see Suzanna shortly. But I felt a part of me was missing. The first time I have ever experienced such an emptiness.

CHAPTER FOURTEEN

I drove to Munich and caught a flight to London Heathrow.

From Terminal Five I took a seat on an airport bus which, eighty minutes later, pulled into the bus station in the centre of Oxford. From there it was a short taxi ride to my parents' home in Norham Gardens, close to University Parks.

My father, Richard, was a lecturer in history and politics at the nearby St Anne's College. He was a man who enjoyed the comforts of life, and expected those around him to smooth his path to a worry-free existence. The true entrance to the College was in the Woodstock Road, which would have entailed an extra quarter of a mile walk; but my mother prevailed upon the college bursar to provide the key to a little-used gated entrance in the Banbury Road, to save him the longer journey.

It appeared my mother, early on in their marriage, had assumed the role of protector and fixer. She came from a noted Austrian family, and was studying at St Anne's when it was an all-female establishment. Even then she was a strong-minded woman; and no doubt, engineered the meeting, the engagement and ultimately the pairing with father. Thus, whenever, a problem loomed, she would quickly step in and steer him away from confrontations, disasters, or family upheavals.

So much so, he was aware he had fathered three children — I had a brother and two sisters — but our growing pains of childhood through to adulthood had eluded him. It was a much-used phrase in the household: `you go up to your study, dear, I'll handle this — small wonder he frequently ascribed the wrong names to me and my siblings.

Mother was the rock in dealing with family matters, and an arch-manipulator on affairs outside the home. It was she, when Angela and I broke up, who declared that I had better come home for a short while until I had sorted myself out. That was three years ago.

Angela had been in the same year as me at Christ Church, where we were both reading History of Art. Looking back, I'm not sure if there were any chemistry between us, more an undemanding inevitability that we would share something of our lives with each other. When she accepted a job with the Courtauld Institute in London, we did not see each other so regularly. More so when I graduated; and, no doubt, with the connivance of my mother, I obtained a junior position with the Kunsthistoriches Museum in Vienna.

After four years I returned to the UK and joined Angela as a live-in partner in her flat in the Richmond suburbs of London. By then my interest in skiing, having been caught up in the sport in Austria since my early teenage years, exceeded my enthusiasm for working in an art gallery.

As often as I could, I would return to the continent to participate in skiing competitions. Eventually, I caught the eye of a leading light and became a member of the British team.

Predictably, this did not fit with the plans Angela had in mind. Gradually, the rift became too wide to support a meaningful relationship. On my twenty-fifth birthday I was handed a card, a matronly kiss on both cheeks, and shown the door.

That's when I moved back to Oxford to lick my not too distressing emotional wounds.

"Hello. . .er, Adam, back I see," remarked my father. "How did you get on?"

"I came fifth in the Downhill at Kitzbühel. Witnessed a nasty accident in a car, and I think, no I hope, I have a new woman in my life."

"Good. That's the spirit."

"Hello darling," said my mother coming into the sitting room and embracing me. "My, you're cold. Sit by the fire I'll bring you in a hot cup of tea and a sandwich."

"Thank you, mother, that would be welcome. The cold in England is different to that in Austria."

"Johann phoned to tell us you came fifth in the Streif. That's a good result. Earned you a lot of FIS points, I should imagine."

Annika, my mother, like her brother Johann, have always been keen skiers, and followed closely the results of the competitions. In fact, my mother was glued to the television whenever the Ski Sunday programmes were on.

Father had left for the college by the time I joined mother at the breakfast table. I gazed out the window at the well-stocked garden, admiring the efforts of my parents, but my thoughts were mostly occupied with Suzanna.

"Who is she, Adam?" she murmured. "Whoever she is must have captured your heart and your mind. You haven`t heard a word I`ve said."

"Sorry. . .you`re right, I have met somebody. She`s one of the British skiing team, her name is Suzanna."

My mother smiled. "How did you meet her?"

"She quite literally knocked me off my feet. When I caught up with the British team in Tignes, she was chasing someone and cannoned into me. In fact, I`m still suffering bruises from the encounter."

"When are you seeing her again?"

"We are skiing in St. Moritz, next week. That`s if I can shake off a twisted ankle I got when witness to an horrific car crash."

"My God, what happened?" mother asked in a concerned voice.

I recounted details of the incident. How a motorist had captured on his dashcam a Mercedes deliberately smashing into a small car, sending it off the road into oblivion.

"The Kia was no match for the larger car. Funnily enough, I had just exchanged a basic, blue Kia for a Volvo. Apparently, Suzanna needs plenty of luggage room."

"What did the Mercedes driver have to say?"

"He didn`t stop, and so far, the police have been unable to trace the car or the owner."

A frown showed on her forehead.

"You said the colour of the car that came off the road was blue. Did I hear you say the Kia you had was blue?" she queried.

"Yes. . .what are you suggesting?"

"Nothing. . .I'm sure it was just coincidence," she exclaimed. "Anyway, coffee, dear? I'll go and make some."

She went to the cupboard to retrieve the coffee machine and concentrated on brewing the coffee. Interesting, she normally makes do with instant.

I could see what she was implying. Had someone made an error, believing I was still driving a Kia. No, surely not. Why would anyone want to harm me?

We sat at the kitchen table, each alone with our thoughts.

Eventually, mother said, "I have to tell you what's on my mind, Adam. Could you have been the intended target? Perhaps, a previous boyfriend of Suzanna, out for revenge at losing her to you. Or a fellow downhill skier upset at beating him in the Streif? I don't know; but from the way you have described the incident, the other car smashing into a blue Kia, and you, having just traded in the same car for a bigger vehicle. . .should I be worried, Adam?"

Father drove me to St. Pancras Station where I caught a Eurostar to the Gare du Nord in Paris. A taxi took me to the Gare de Lyon, and a TVG — Lyria high-speed train whisked me to Zurich in just four hours.

After that, things slowed down.

It took the same amount of time from Zurich to St. Moritz.

A long journey, but it gave me time to think about my mother's remarks. Could she be right? Was someone trying to injure me, to take me out of the skiing game? At the moment I wasn't a threat to the big names; but maybe in the future? I liked to think so. When I catch up with Josh Finden, I'll get his opinion.

A room had been booked for me at the Crystal Hotel.

As usual, Josh Finden had chosen well.

It was close to the funicular railway which takes competitors up the Corviglia where we change to the gondolas for the final leg to the start of the Downhill.

My mobile phone chirped. It was Suzanna.

"Where are you?" she asked.

"About forty minutes away from St. Moritz. And you?"

"I'm already here, at the Crystal Hotel. That's where we are all staying. Can you hang on a moment?" Her voice dropped to a whisper.

A minute passed.

"That's better. I've moved away from the others. Adam, I've got a favour to ask. Is it possible I can share your room with you? That bloody Todd said to me when we were boarding the minibus, by the way, you won't be wanting your bedroom will you? So I've allocated it to Phyllis, our physio. She can use it as a treatment room. What a damned cheek!"

"I am delighted! Naturally, you can. I was hoping that might be the case."

"But it's so presumptuous on his part!"

"Well, I guess, by now, everyone in the team knows about us."

She giggled. "Yes, I suppose so. Anyway, see you in half an hour."

There was a tap on the door.

I opened it to find Suzanna, and a porter struggling with two cases and a holdall. I despatched him with a tip and closed the door. As I turned Suzanna put her arms round my neck and kissed me, long and hard.

"Wow, that really was something," she said huskily.

My heart was thumping, and I stared at her with a half-smile on my lips. Never, in all the relationships I have enjoyed, and at times endured, has any woman taken the initiative so boldly. It was a pleasing revelation.

"By the way I forgot to ask," I muttered, lying on the bed with Suzanna, "when is your Super G?"

"Not until Wednesday. Why?"

"I've got you a little something. It just might help when you check out the course and the gates."

"Really? What is it?"

I got up and went to my holdall, delved in a side pocket and handed her a package.

"It's this, a small recorder. As you ski alongside the course you can record all the details. Then you can play it back to yourself until it's fixed in your mind."

"What a good idea, Adam. That's brilliant. Will you come with me, as you did in Garmisch?"

"Of course. I'll be by your side as long as you want me to be."

She raised an eyebrow and grinned. The remark came as much a surprise to Suzanna as it did to me. In the past, I have murmured endearments to girlfriends, but in a light-hearted way. This was the first time such a signal of my true feelings had ever been expressed.

"Well that's comforting, to have your input on the slopes," she exclaimed, passing off the comment. But it had been declared, and I wondered how she would take it.

She leaned forward, squeezed my hand, and kissed me on the cheek.

We spent a full hour together assessing the Super G run.

Then at twelve o`clock the race began.

Suzanna took her place at the starting gate at a quarter to one. I was feeling on edge, and walked away from the other team members, willing her to have a clear picture in her mind of the course and the gates.

Even at a distance I could see Suzanna was out the gate and increasing her speed with each stab of the poles. She was executing a perfect line at each of the gates, jumping well, tucking in to maintain balance and minimise drag, yet she finished seventh. Something wasn`t right.

I made my way to skiers` exit and waited for her to emerge.

When she removed her helmet there were tears in her eyes, and she held on to me confirming something was amiss.

"What is it, darling? What`s wrong?"

She sniffed. "Blue. . .you said in Garmisch the wrecked car was blue. . . at the time it didn`t register. When I started my run I was suddenly aware the marker flags at the gates were blue. I was skiing between course lines that were blue. And the colour of your Kia. . .blue! My God, were you the intended victim, not the hapless fellow killed in the accident? That`s all I could think of. Hang the Super G! Don`t you dare let yourself be taken from me!"

This time she held me in such a tight grip I could scarcely breathe. It was several minutes before we broke apart.

I murmured in her ear, "Todd is on his way over, don't repeat what you've just said. Let's talk later."

"What, Anatoly Vasiliev the jumper? The one who died at Bischofshofen?"

I had explained to Suzanna that the only item of slight concern was his request to discuss something with me. Something he had seen in Lucerne.

I also mentioned that, as I comforted Anatoly on the jump course, with almost his last breath he had mouthed two words, 'microswitch' and 'UPS'.

"Microswitch and the initials of the United Parcel Service. What on earth did he mean?" asked Suzanna.

"Unfortunately, the words meant nothing to me," I replied.

"But he was anxious to talk to you? Could they be the key to a secret, and he was killed before he could tell you what it was?"

"Aren't you being a little melodramatic? It was an accident. A binding came apart, and he lost a ski. When you are that high, crashing to earth can be fatal. . .as it was with poor Anatoly."

"Perhaps it was made to appear an accident?" she said worriedly.

"The coroner's report declared it was accidental. These things happen. Everyone knows the risk. When I was in England for a few days, my mother had similar thoughts. I told her not to read too much into the car incident. Yes, it was deliberate, knocking the Kia off the road, but there's no way the driver could have thought it was me."

"What do you mean, your mother voiced the same

thoughts, but you dismissed the idea? Do you realise that she and I could be right! Face facts, Adam!"

"OK, let`s say you`re right," I shrugged. "So what do I do. . .hide? Find a hole to crawl into? What do you suggest? Go to the police? Tell them someone is trying to kill me?"

Suzanna stared at me. Her mouth tightened, eventually she said. "OK, you can`t tell the police, there`s no real evidence to go on. Perhaps, it`s just womanly intuition. . .but your mother and I can`t both be wrong. So I`m going to make damned sure you`re careful. I`m going to be right by your side all the time."

I grinned at her. "All the time? Now that`s an offer I gladly accept!"

Before the course was closed to the public Suzanna came with me when I checked out the Downhill starting gate. I had skied the course on a number of occasions, and was aware how precipitous are the first one hundred and fifty metres. When you leave the gate the slope literally drops away. You are almost falling. It is so steep, that you accelerate to a hundred and forty kilometres an hour in just six seconds. A shade quicker than a Porsche 911 Carrera. Although the start of the course is termed, `Free Fall`, most competitors enjoy the adrenalin rush you get when you push through the gate. Although you are travelling at speed, your first turn is a left-hander which you have to judge carefully to avoid running wide.

What I did not mention to Suzanna when we left the gondola was the metal staircase to the official start hut.

"My God, do we have to climb there?"

"Yes, afraid so, all one hundred and eighty-seven

steps. You carry your own skis in practice, though come race day, a porter carries them up there for you."

At the top Suzanna admired the view, but couldn't bring herself to come closer to the edge. "This is seriously dangerous, Adam. One false move skiing down there and you'd be in trouble!"

"Actually, Suzanna, it's not nearly as bad as it seems, as long as you stay on your feet. To my mind, technically, the Streif is a harder run. The St Moritz course is open all the way down, whereas in Kitzbühel trees grow alongside the course; and there are several blind jumps that make landing difficult."

She was not convinced. "Can we go down now?"

I had retrieved my gear from the mini-bus, and passed the skis to one of Josh's people to check the edges and wax them.

The next two days were devoted to practice, or training as the International Ski Federation term it. Important, for your timing decides where you ski in the final group of thirty racers.

On the second day, when it was my turn to ease forward to the starting gate, I placed my poles over the wand and took two deep breaths. On the third, I pushed out, and was away. My speed on the steepest slope in competition skiing took me quickly to well over eighty miles an hour. I breathed out coming into the left-hand turn, a slight drag on the left pole, and held my line, still maintaining speed off the Free Fall.

Besides appearing on the big screen, Suzanna had binoculars trained on me. I brushed past several gate markers, started a side slip too early coming up to one on an adverse bend, but managed to clear the gate.

I was exhilarated by the momentum. Yes, there were heart-in-the-mouth moments. Particularly towards the end of the run when I came to the infamous `Rominger Jump`.

It is not a high jump, but it is long and seems to go on for ever. In a tuck position, my leg muscles were screaming by the time I bounced back onto the snow a little untidily, and catapulted through the arch of the finish line.

One minute, thirty-nine, point one five!

Seventh place!

Suzanna greeted me before Todd and the others came over.

"Wow! That was brilliant, Adam!" she exclaimed, wrapping her arms around my neck before I could remove my helmet.

"Let go of him, Suzanna, let the chap breathe," called Todd, shaking my gloved hand. "Do that in the final, and I can see a podium finish," he added. "Where do you think you can lose a few fractions of a second?"

At that moment Josh joined us. He did not say much other than `well done` and patted me on the back. He turned to his companion. "Ron, take Adam`s skis and put them in tip-top racing mode."

I handed them to the fellow, a short, wiry individual, who sported tattoos on both hands; and, from what I could see, a serpent`s head showed slightly above the collar of his anorak.

My thoughts turned to shedding those hundredths of a second.

"I slowed slightly coming off the `Free Fall`, turning into the lefthander. Perhaps a little there, and possibly the

Rominger Jump. It wasn't a good landing, I could try to improve my tuck, though I was aware my legs were gradually dropping with fatigue."

Another competitor pushed me back to eighth; but still in the first top ten of skiers, which meant, if I drew a good bib number, I would have the best of conditions with minimal rutting of the snow.

I awoke to the sound of my mobile chirping.

"I've just heard from Johann that you were eighth in training, which puts you're in the first ten," exclaimed my mother. "That's fantastic, Adam. What time is the Downhill? Will you phone me once you've finished? I'm so excited for you. . .give it your best shot." Then she added, "but don't take too many risks."

"I shan't. I'll be careful, don't worry. I've been working with Todd to see where I can improve my time without courting danger."

"Well make sure you listen to him, and don't forget to phone me. Good luck, Adam, I shall be cheering for you at this end. God bless."

"Who was that?" came a voice from somewhere under the duvet. It was a rest day, and we were being lazy.

"My mother. She's a keen skier, and is much into the sport, like the rest of her Austrian family."

"Oh, I didn't know she was Austrian. Is that why you speak German so fluently?"

"Well, in Vienna, where my Mother's family live, they have a city accent," I explained. "It's quite different from Hochdeutsch, and while I can adapt to and speak High German, I prefer the more melodic tone of Viennese.

"It`s odd in a way," I continued, "because of the manner in which we speak, Germans think Austrians are pleasant people, but slightly quaint and old-fashioned. Whereas the Austrians consider Germans to be humourless, arrogant and inflexible."

"Well, could you use your best Hochdeutsch and order up some breakfast, I`m starving," declared Suzanna.

St. Moritz is expensive. I thought Suzanna knew that when someone advised her to visit the Palace Galerie where she would find exactly the shoes she was keen to buy.

"I saw them in a magazine in Tignes, and I just have to have them," she announced. "Will you come with me? I don`t speak German, and you can explain what I`m looking for."

I didn`t comment that St. Moritz is so cosmopolitan, whatever language you speak someone was sure to understand. So I tagged along. Happily not for long. I had to say the shoes did suit her, and I had the feeling she would have worn them for the rest of the day, had not the price been mentioned. They were quickly removed and returned to the sales assistant. Suzanna was still fulminating at the `ridiculous cost of the pair of shoes, which she could buy in London for half the price`, when I steered her into Hanselmann`s coffee house on Via Maistra.

Several tables away I noticed Josh Finden with two of his clients, Greg Nichols and Mark Williams, an American. I had seen both Greg`s and Mark`s names on the list of competitors when registering for the Downhill, and thought I would introduce myself.

"I won't be a minute, I'll just say hello to Josh," I said, pushing back my chair.

They were deep in conversation when I arrived at their table. Greg looked up, annoyed at someone was hovering by them. It took a moment for him to recognise me.

Josh was quicker. "Well, look who's here," he exclaimed. Then he glanced round and saw Suzanna. "My dear," he called waving an arm, "come and join us. Get two more chairs will you, Greg?"

I shook Mark William's hand. "Adam Livesey, pleased to meet you. And this is Suzanna Bancroft, also on the British team."

He smiled warmly in her direction and rose to his feet. "Have my chair, Suzanna."

"My, the perfect gentleman, how nice," she murmured, as he eased her chair towards the table.

Chatting about the various races, snow quality, the event timings, and the season thus far, time drifted towards lunchtime, and we all decided to eat in the coffee house.

It was well after three o'clock when we went our different ways. Despite the annoyance at not buying the shoes Suzanna had so much admired, she still wanted to buy a few other items; so we returned to the main shopping area in La Via Serias in search of a leather belt.

I left her for a short while, while she dithered over which of two she might purchase. Fifteen minutes later, when I returned, she was still at the counter trying to come to a decision. Eventually, Suzanna had neither, much to the assistant's suppressed chagrin.

We were back in the hotel room when there was a discreet tap on the door.

"You open it," I said, looking out the window towards

the heights of the Corviglia.

"It`s your room," Suzanna muttered, marching towards the door. She flung it open intimidating the messenger boy, who started to back away.

"Miss Bancroft?" he said in an uncertain voice. "This was delivered ten minutes ago."

He thrust a parcel into her hands, and fled down the corridor.

Suzanna slowly closed the door, and sat in a chair staring at the package. "I wonder what it is," she murmured. "I haven`t bought or ordered anything."

"Why don`t you open it and find out. . .it might be from an admirer."

"Nobody knows I`m here. . .well in this room," she said, still staring at the object now residing on the coffee table. "I don`t see how anyone could discover my actual whereabouts."

Suzanna lent forward and untied the decorative bow. Then she carefully began removing the outer wrapping. Suddenly, a thought struck her, and she tore feverishly at the remaining layers, until the lid of a square box was revealed.

Slowly she lifted the lid, and gasped. "My God. . .the shoes I so wanted." She turned round to me. "So that`s where you went this afternoon. I wondered what you were up to."

With that, Suzanna jumped up and rushed towards me. Unlike the messenger boy I knew what to expect. But even I found it hard to resist the frontal assault, and we fell together on the bed.

We were late for dinner that evening.

Suzanna wore her new shoes, and I, well I wore a satisfied smile.

CHAPTER FIFTEEN

Race day.

Nestled into the cliff face high above the old start, the `Free Fall` is the steepest start on the World Cup tour, with racers reaching speeds around 130 kmh, well over eighty miles an hour, in seconds.

Skiing at speed while negotiating the demanding twists and turns requires careful preparation. I was determined not to hesitate on the left-hander after the gradient nor on the steep Suvretta Edge.

Racers who win the Downhill in St Moritz are those who use the terrain instead of fighting it. They maintain their speed after Free Fall over the rolls, jumps, and blind corners.

Moreover, they know how to fly. Over the three-kilometre course up to three hundred metres is spent in the air.

Then the Mauer Wall can make or break your race. This section begins at about one minute and fifteen seconds into the descent, when the tuck position is punishing your legs, and there's still another thirty seconds to ski.

There's a jump leading into two completely blind

turns followed by a sharp right-foot fall-away turn. Exiting the Mauer Wall, and then the Felsen Bend, it's critical for racers to get the combination right.

All one has to do now, when confronting the Rominger Jump, is to sail through the air for up to eighty metres; and almost immediately afterwards to clear the Lärchensprung and hold the tuck until you cross the finish line.

I joined Greg and Mark in the funicular, we were in the same gondola conveying us to the heights. Before climbing the metal staircase to the starting hut, I briefly checked the underside of my skis. Ron, Josh`s technician, had seemingly done a good job. Sharp edges and nicely waxed.

At the top I waited with other racers in the nearby hospitality building until I was called forward.

"Good luck, Adam," called Mark. "And contrary to theatre people, don`t break a leg."

I smiled, as I put on the helmet and made my way to the start.

I stood behind several skiers awaiting their turn; and watched them mentally rehearse the run, gently swaying this way and that as the course unfolded in their minds.

One of them disappeared from view as he broke the wand and leapt down the Free Fall.

Then the fellow in front of me was gone. I inched forward, until I was on the start line and poles over the wand. The starter counted down, `four, three, two, one. . .and I was flying, almost literally.

In the past few days perhaps I had treated the downhill lightly. Another mountain, another patch of snow — another occasion to enjoy the thrill of racing. But this was different, I was urging myself on, shouting as I reached for maximum velocity.

The left-hander was coming up, did I dare to take it at the flood and ignore the growing uncertainties as I hurtled down the run.

My left pole dropped slightly, ready to slacken speed.

Heart in my mouth I lifted it clear of the snow.

I was pushed wide, but not much off the racing line. Now I was charging. The course opened up for me. Another left turn; a heart-stopping jump; two right-handers, a host of reverse camber turns; another jump then a depression; and suddenly, looming up, the Rominger Jump.

In my mind the only thought was, do it right and the time would surely put me in the top ten. Then I was soaring. I dropped my hands and held the tuck regardless of the desperate need to straighten my legs. It seemed to go on forever.

The ground came up to meet me.

I knew it would be a hard landing, but so close to the finish I was sure my remaining strength would carry me over the line.

I hit the snow, the left binding released, the ski pirouetted into the air. I veered off course into the netting at speed, at such an angle I bounced off the safety barrier and tumbled further down the slope.

I came to rest on my back, and wondered why the world around me appeared to be receding. My vision was fast disappearing through a smaller and smaller hole until it closed completely. Awareness gradually shut down. I lapsed into unconsciousness.

CHAPTER SIXTEEN

I could hear the sound of people speaking.

Sometimes nearby, at other times indistinct and far away.

My hand was gripped, and I sensed a kiss on my forehead. Shadows and shapes moved around me; but the effort to find out what they were was too much. . .they simply faded away.

There they were again. Why do these vague outlines and dismembered voices invade my consciousness. Make them go away. Leave me in peace, I crave the solitude.

Something brushed my forehead. It felt soft. The feeling lingered. What was it? Suddenly, I had to find out. I opened my eyes.

Suzanna was leaning over me. When she saw me staring at her she burst into tears.

A man in a white coat moved her aside and said. "Welcome back to the land of the living, Herr Livesey. Can you understand what I'm saying?"

"Welcome to the land of, or something much like it," I croaked. My mouth was dry, my tongue so swollen I could hardly enunciate the words.

"Let me arrange for some water, Herr Livesey," the fellow said, and left the room.

"Where am I, Suzanna?" I managed to say. What was I doing in this white-walled, sparsely furnished room with a machine on a stand discreetly bleeping. I looked down at my body, an array of tubes led from the machine under the bedclothes and were clearly connected to various parts of me. Further down my legs appeared to be covered by a frame.

"You're in the Klinik Exzellenz in St. Moritz," she explained. "An ambulance rushed you here when you had the accident,"

The memory off crashing at speed flooded back. My left binding had given way on landing after the Rominger Jump.

A carafe of water arrived. Greedily, I gulped it down, and was immediately assailed by a wave of nausea, a reaction obvious to the nurse.

"You should not drink it so quickly, otherwise you'll be sick," she chided, when I recovered.

"Ring if you want anything," she added leaving the room.

Suzanne moved from a chair to sit on the edge of the bed, and held my hand. "Am I glad to see you open your eyes and at least appear, to be normal," she said smiling. "Actually, until you came round they didn't know if you had suffered any brain injury. The chief surgeon did say they would test for abnormalities. I told him he would find plenty. Anyone who skis at breakneck speed down mountains cannot be right in the head."

I nodded and gave a feeble grin.

"Suzanna, can you help me?" I managed to say. Dosed with drugs I knew my speech was slurred.

99

"Of course, what is it you want?"

"My skis. In particular the left one, where the binding was activated," I mumbled.

"No problem. I collected both skis and they are in our room at the hotel, together with the rest of your gear."

She looked into my eyes. I saw tenderness. . .and something else. Was it love, or just concern for a fellow skier? Any other thoughts were suddenly dispelled when she leant forward and kissed me hard. When she drew back her eyes were moist. Her voice cracked when she said, "I thought I`d lost you. Don`t you ever put me through the wringer like that again!"

I tried to put my arms around her, but only one responded to the effort.

The other I realised was hindered by substantial strapping.

"What sort of damage have I suffered; do you know?"

"Enough to keep you off skis for a while," Suzanna promptly remarked.

I was about to quiz her, to learn the true state of my injuries, when the fellow in the white coat appeared again. This time he had a stethoscope around his neck and a more serious air about him.

"Herr Livesey, you are a lucky man," he announced, dropping into a bedside chair. "By the way, my name is Grimwald, Hans Grimwald, your physician. I see a lot of skiing accidents, mostly holidaymakers who are in St Moritz for the snow and the après-ski. The professionals, like yourself, are not regular patients; but when they are they tend to do more damage to themselves, particularly downhill racers."

He crossed his legs and settled back in the chair.

"I have to say, on this occasion, you appear to have

sustained tourist-level injuries. There's a suggestion of a mild fracture of the right shoulder, heavily bruised ribs, and lacerations to both legs," he explained. "However, my main concern was the possibility of brain damage. Your helmet came off when you tumbled down the slope, and you clearly suffered concussion with the considerable likelihood of intracranial haemorrhage. We did an emergency CT scan, and it would appear you got away lightly. No bleeding just a shake-up. But for a while you may suffer headaches, some severe, before things settle down."

He turned to Suzanna. "We'll keep him in overnight, and your husband can be discharged tomorrow. Can you make sure you take good care of him for the next few weeks."

She did not bat an eyelid at our supposed relationship. "That won't be a problem, doctor," Suzanna confirmed. "I won't let him out of my sight. I'll make sure he behaves."

"Now we come to the question of settlement," he remarked, turning back to me. "Our admin department will provide an itemised invoice, and presumably you have some form of professional sportsman's medical cover."

"Yes, it's with the Luzerner Krankenkasse, but I can't recall the policy number."

"Not a problem, our administrative people will get in touch with them, and sort it out. All we shall ask of you is the excess charge. Well, that's everything." Grimwald added, "I'll check you over before you leave, and set up your release. See you in the morning."

With that he bowed in Suzanna's direction, and swept from the room.

"Obviously the concussion erased all memory of our wedding," I grinned at Suzanna. "Was it a quickie, five minutes in front of a bribed registrar?"

She looked slightly abashed when she murmured, "They would only allow close relatives to be by your side I had to say something. . . being your wife was the first thing I could think of."

"Wow, from close encounters of the bruising kind, to marriage in just a few weeks, must be some kind of record," I said smiling.

"I don't think that's very funny," Suzanna said smarting from my remark. "I was concerned for you, Adam. As you now appear to be your usual sarcastic self, I'm leaving. I'll share Phyllis' hotel room, and you can have your bedroom all to yourself!"

She turned towards the door.

"Suzanna, wait! I don't want you to leave. Look, I'm sorry. . .perhaps I was too flippant."

But she was undeterred, and was reaching for the door handle when I tried to get out of bed to stop her. One step, and I staggered. The second step and I was sinking. Overcome by a wave of giddiness and nausea, I collapsed to the floor.

Several nurses had anxious looks on their faces, and Grimwald was stony-faced as he examined me. "Don't try to get out of bed again. You are to stay here for at least another day before you can be discharged, do you understand?"

I nodded carefully, in case the dizziness returned.

The most distressed was Suzanna. She was the other side of the bed clutching my hand.

When the others trooped out the room, she murmured.

"I`m so sorry, Adam. . .it was all my fault," she murmured. "I should have realised you might do something stupid like that. Anyway, I would not have gone far, I can`t leave you in your present state."

"What about when my state improves?"

She smiled. "Perhaps then, if you are able to look after yourself."

I felt my heart lurch.

"What if I wanted a full-time carer? What if I also cared for you? Would you stay then?"

"An interesting question," she said, looking into my eyes. "I need time to think about it. . .OK, I`ve thought about it, the answer is yes," Suzanna replied with a smile.

"Wonderful!"

In the late afternoon Suzanna returned to the hotel. She had been my constant companion for the last few days, and was now going to freshen up and enjoy a good meal.

"I`ll come back about nine o`clock to the check on you. . . ensure you are behaving yourself," she said lightly. "By the way, phone your parents, tell them you`re all right. If they follow the fortunes of skiing, they`ll be worried for you."

When the phone was answered by my father, my normal reaction was to say `could you put mother on the line`. But we chatted for a few minutes, and for once he seemed genuinely interested in what I was doing.

When, eventually, he passed over the phone, mother immediately said, "My God, Adam, what have you been up to? I`ve just seen the recorded highlights of the St.

Moritz Downhill. Are you alright?"

"Yes, Mother, it looked worse than it is in reality. The usual bruises, nothing to worry about."

"When I hadn`t heard from you I was all for catching the next plane," she said with a catch in her voice.

"No problems, Mother. In fact, we`re off to Aspen next for the tournament. I`ll keep in touch."

After another brief exchange I rang off.

A few hours later, I was feeling pleasantly tired, when there was a tap on the door. It opened slowly, and the head and shoulders of Alexei Sokolov appeared.

"May I come in, Adam?" he enquired.

"Of course, my friend. It`s nice to see you. But what are you doing in St. Moritz? Is your patron here as well?"

Alexei laughed. "No he is still on the Black Sea, enjoying the sea air and the favours of his mistress. I left them to it and escaped to Zauberberg Semmering for some free-riding on the slopes. At least that was my intention. At the hotel in Vienna I caught your accident on television, and thought I should come to St. Moritz to see how my good friend was faring."

"Well that was decent of you, Alexei. How did you get here from Vienna?"

"I took a charter flight to Bolzano and hired a car to bring me here," Alexei explained.

A good friend, yes. . .but why did he go to that expense when a phone call would have sufficed? He must have seen the uncertainty on my face.

"Look, Adam, I have a confession to make. Naturally, I would want to know how you were, but at the back of my mind was also the thought you might be able to help me."

"Really, Alexei, how could I do that?"

"Are you going to Sochi for the forthcoming tournament? I realise you won't be skiing, but I know members of the British team are competing, and you may be accompanying them."

"As a matter of fact, that was my intention. You see. . ."

The door opened and Suzanna came into the room.

She nodded to Alexei, kissed me on the forehead, and turned again to Alexei, awaiting an introduction.

"Darling, this is Alexei Sokolov. Alexei, this is Suzanna Bancroft. She is the British Super G champion, and also someone very dear to me."

They shook hands. "Adam, has often mentioned you, Alexei. You met on the Semmering slopes, I believe," said Suzanna.

Alexei gave a wry smile.

"More a collision, Suzanna," he replied.

"When you arrived," I remarked, "Alexei was querying whether I would be at Sochi for the tournament. I shall certainly be there to cheer on Suzanna in the Super G, and, of course, others in the British team. So, how could I help you, my friend?"

"I think I had better give you the background to my request."

For the next half hour Sokolov told us of the man to whom he was chief aid. He recounted the demands made upon him by the president, and spoke of the audacity of Tupolev's new neighbour, building on an adjacent promontory and blocking much of the view to the sea.

He, Sokolov, had been charged with dissuading the Mafia boss from building his summer retreat. That was a continuing problem. Of more immediate concern was the problem of smuggling back to Moscow, Olga Petrova, Tupolev`s mistress and well-known Russian film actress. It was vital she not be recognised. According to his boss, the good name of the president must be preserved at all costs.

"How specifically, can I help you, Alexei?" I asked.

"This is what I have in mind, Adam."

Two days later I was back in our room at the Crystal Hotel.

I was able to walk without feeling dizzy, or my legs suddenly giving way. On the occasions my head ached, I took the pills prescribed by Grimwald, the physician at the Klinik Exzellenz.

Most of the British skiers called by to see me, and predictably, I made light of crashing out of the Downhill. Like horseracing jockeys, professional skiers tend to exhibit a greater tolerance to pain and minor injury, rarely talk of their mishaps, and are known for their bodies to heal quickly. When I told them I would be back on skis very shortly, I genuinely believed I would.

First, though, I had to discover why the binding of the left ski released.

While I was receiving visitors, Suzanna was busy trying to find my skis, which Todd Stewart had taken from her and stowed in the team`s equipment room in the hotel basement. They had since disappeared.

"I wasn`t prepared to give up that easily," she

declared.

Undaunted, she had asked other coaches if the skis had inadvertently been taken into any of their storerooms. They allowed her to check, but the skis were not found.

Some hours later, the Crystal Hotel staff must have wondered what this strange woman was up to when she requested access to the rubbish bins' compound. Eventually, they agreed to her venturing into unseen parts of the hotel accompanied by one of the porters. He led her through the boiler room, along pipe-lined corridors, through the laundry and storage areas to the back of the building. Opening a well-fortified door, they emerged at the same time as a refuse collection vehicle arrived.

"I made them wait while I lifted the lids of the large, four-wheel bins, and poked around the innards," she recounted. "There was a great deal of muttering about the delay I was causing, but the third bin yielded the prize," Suzanna said triumphantly, brandishing the remnants of my left ski.

"It has clearly been broken up to get it in the bin, and to disguise the fact it belongs to you," she added. "But the critical section, the binding, is in one piece."

I walked over, put my arms around her waist and kissed her.

"I am amazed at your tenacity," I murmured. "I doubt I would have thought to look amongst the refuse."

I took the broken ski and placed it on the coffee table.

"Now, let's see what this reveals."

I stood there for a moment contemplating the binding. In a way it's a misnomer. The term conjures up a strap device to secure your feet to the ski. In reality, these days a binding is a metal undersole attached to the ski into which your boot is secured both back and front. Importantly, to minimise injury, the mechanism will release the boot when a skier falls or on impact.

The release can be set for the level of ability. If you are a cautious to moderate skier you don`t need a high setting. For the more aggressive skier, such as a professional, you set the release for the highest setting, which also takes into account your height, weight, and ski-boot-sole length. A technician will take note all these factors when preparing your skis. Thereafter, the settings are only checked when skis are overhauled, though the edges and waxing are made ready for every run.

"Well, anything out of the ordinary?" asked Suzanna.

I peered closely at the setting.

"No wonder the ski fell away upon impact after the Rominger Jump! The release setting has been altered! It was set to operate when I landed heavily just before the finish. Look. . .it is a much lower setting," I said, pointing to the adjustment.

"Who would do such a thing?"

"The question is more who could do such a thing! Only a knowledgeable technician. . .such as Josh`s man, Ron!" I exclaimed.

He was on the slopes with his clients.

It was late afternoon before I made contact with Josh on his cell phone.

"Hello."

"Josh, it`s Adam."

"Nice to hear your voice, my friend. How are things? Are you on the mend? Is that gorgeous nurse of yours adding blood pressure to your list of ailments?"

He laughed at the remark. I was too incensed to find it amusing.

"I'm looking for Ron, your technician, Josh. He's not in the hotel, do you know where he is?"

"You and me both, Adam. I can't find him either. He was supposed to prepare Mark's skis, but he has simply disappeared. I searched for him early this morning, but he was nowhere to be found. Why do you want him?"

"Are you eating in the hotel this evening?"

"Yes, we've had a tough day. . .little need for celebrations."

"OK if Suzanna and I join you? I'll explain then."

None of Josh's clients, nor any members of the British team, myself included, had covered ourselves in glory; and when Suzanna and I arrived at the table we were met by gloomy faces. Moments later Lars Oestensson appeared.

Josh turned to me. "I've got some good news Adam. Lars has just appointed me as his agent, so you'll be seeing a lot more of each other in the future."

I nodded in Lars's direction, but I cannot say I warmed to the thought.

"What brings you to an Alpine tournament, Lars, there's no cross-country here?" asked Suzanna, greeting him with a warm smile.

"It was an opportunity to sign up with Josh, and to meet the rest of his entourage," he replied. "Also, I'm venturing more towards Alpine skiing, concentrating on the Super G."

It was towards the end of the meal, when coffee was

being served, that the opportunity to speak with Josh arose. Greg Nichols left an empty chair when he went to the restroom, and I moved round the table and sat in it.

"So what`s the great need to speak with Ron Grainger all about?" he queried.

"Presumably, he set up my skis for the downhill training run?"

Josh Finden nodded. "Of course, usually he does for all our skiers."

"Then listen carefully to what I have to tell you. Losing a ski after the Rominger Jump was no accident," I said icily. "Your man, Ron, deliberately adjusted the binding to pop when I made the hard landing on the last jump!"

"He wouldn`t do that!" protested Josh.

The whole table went quiet. Suddenly, everyone was listening to our exchanges.

"He was in charge of the skis. He prepared them for competition. Only Ron Grainger had the opportunity to recalibrate those release settings. . .no one else."

"An unfair accusation, Adam! Ron is not here to defend himself," declared Finden, glaring at me.

"Exactly! So why isn`t he here? Probably because I survived," I added. "I`ll wager he won`t turn up again."

"Adam, I just can`t believe what you are saying. Ron has worked for me for seven years. I know I can rely on him. Wherever he is, he`ll be here tomorrow morning, you`ll see."

There was an uneasy silence around the table.

Suzanna said quietly, "Time for your medication, Adam. You shouldn`t ignore the schedule. I`ll come up to your room shortly, to make sure you you`re observing doctor`s orders."

She had that look in her eye I was only just beginning to recognise.

I pushed back the chair. "If you'll excuse me everyone, I need to take some pills."

Suzanna appeared thirty minutes later.

"Well?"

"Darling, I suggested you took your medication before either Josh or you created a gap so wide it could never be breached. When the heat of the moment had cooled, I told them all that had happened in a calm, measured fashion.

"Firstly, I presumed the skiers who had competed today had trouble-free runs. When they nodded or agreed in so many words, I then told all at the table how your skis were eventually taken into the equipment room after the accident. Yet when I went to retrieve them, the left ski was missing.

"I mentioned my thorough search of the hotel, checking every possible location to find the missing ski. Guess where I found it, I said. The look on all their faces when I told them, one of the hotel's refuse bins. Moreover, it had been chopped into three, and dumped in the bottom of the bin. To my mind, I said, there was no possible doubt it was deliberate, and the culprit could only have been Ron Grainger. Examining the remnant of the ski holding the binding, it was all too obvious the release tension had been altered.

"Let's face it, I said, Adam could so easily have been killed. Only one conclusion can be drawn. This incident, along with a few others, were callous attempts to rid the world of Adam Livesey. I will not stand by and let it happen. With that I walked out the restaurant."

"I`ll bet that shut them up," I remarked.

"Quite the contrary. The buzz of conversation when I left was at fever pitch."

I sat up, grabbing Suzanna by the waist I pulled her towards me — and that`s where it ended. I twisted my injured shoulder, let out a howl of pain and fell backwards onto the bed.

CHAPTER SEVENTEEN

The next morning, when Suzanna and I were walking towards the breakfast room, a porter handed me a letter. The only inscription on the face of the envelope was Herr A Livesey, Crystal Hotel.

At that moment Josh Finden appeared, and the three of us moved to a distant table.

"Look Adam, I want to apologise for my behaviour last night," he murmured.

"I was about to say the same thing," I replied. "I chose the wrong moment to make such comments. I should have known better."

He smiled, "It seems you were right. After you had gone to your room, Suzanna here put me in the picture about searching for the missing ski. Moreover, Grainger has not turned up. It looks as though he has skedaddled before the authorities caught up with him. What he did was criminal."

It suddenly came to me that Suzanna had been right to send me away last night. If I had stayed much longer I would have lost a well-respected agent; and recounting the details of her search for the ski in a cool, calm manner had clearly allowed Josh, and the others at the table, to come to terms with the fact that Ron Grainger had cold-bloodedly set out to finish me off.

Back in our room we were packing to leave when I suddenly remembered the envelope I had stuffed into a pocket. Opening it I found it was from the administration department at the Klinik Exzellenz requesting I phone them.

Moments later I learned that the medical insurance company, Luzerner Krankenkasse, had paid far less than their policy stipulated, and the excess, which I had to pay, had been substantially increased. Would I pay the Klinik Exzellenz the outstanding extra sums?

I agreed to do so, and immediately thereafter phoned the insurance company, only to be told that they could, at any time, propose a greater amount to be paid by the client. Not without out prior consultation I reminded them.

The individual on the other end of the line, besides being insistent that the company would not pay a penny more, was dismissive, almost arrogant in his attitude.

Angrily, I slammed down the phone. "Who do they think they are?" I declared. "A contract is a contract, they can't alter the terms just like that."

"Why don't you go and sort them out," said Suzanna. "Lucerne is no great distance away. I can drive you there, and afterwards we can make our way leisurely to Tignes. That's if you are going to Tignes. Are you heading anywhere else?"

"I'm going where you're going," I smiled. "After all, I can't drive yet, so I'm in your hands."

"Good. . .so strip off, it's time for a little gentle massage before we hit the road."

"I've been thinking," I remarked, as Suzanna's

soothing hands eased my chest and shoulder. "Anatoly Vasiliev wanted to tell me something about what he saw in Lucerne. At the time he was standing on the steps of the Grand Hotel on Haldenstrasse. Do you remember, he murmured two words before he died, `microswitch` and `UPS`."

"Why don`t you book us a room at the Grand Hotel? If we stand on the steps, we might catch what he saw."

According to the Satnav in the car the journey to Lucerne was two hundred and twenty-five kilometres — approximately a hundred and fifty miles on a good road.

About halfway we stopped for lunch at a restaurant called Gasthaus zum Schiff. Not only was the food good, but the views across Lake Zurich were enchanting.

We arrived at the Grand late afternoon, and I decided to tackle the insurance company first thing the next morning.

"Interesting," I remarked, as we unpacked. "The insurance company address is Haldensteig, so it won`t be too far away."

"`Strasse` is street, isn`t it?" commented Suzanna. "So what is a `steig`?"

"It translates as `track` or `path`. Most likely, it will be a turning close by."

In fact, the concierge pointed it out to us. It was almost opposite the hotel entrance, and visible from the hotel steps. Waiting for a lull in the traffic we crossed Haldenstrasse and walked up the narrow roadway towards the entrance of a large building.

On the wall, either side of glass, double doors, were the nameplates of a number of businesses. In all there were about a dozen organisations housed in its interior.

Luzerner Krankenkasse was on the third floor. We were directed to the lifts by the receptionist in the entrance hall, and met by a man in his forties, neatly, but conservatively dressed in a dark suit and maroon tie displaying the company's initials, L and K, entwined as a gold motif.

"Good morning, may I help you?" was said in a Berlin dialect.

"I believe so," I responded. "Here are the details of my policy number, I want to discuss a recent claim I am making on the company."

"I see, please come this way," said the fellow imperiously.

We followed him as he hurried along the corridor.

"Adam, I've just seen the letters, `UPS` on a door?" Suzanna whispered.

"Where?" I asked, stopping suddenly.

"It's on a piece of card hanging on that door handle." She pointed to a door we had just passed.

"UPS`. . .I wonder if that's what Vasiliev was referring to? Interesting. . .let's catch up with our friend."

We were shown into a small, bare interview room.

"My colleague, Herr Schmidt, will attend to you shortly," was the parting comment.

Ten minutes passed, neither of us said a word. Eventually, a clone of the previous fellow appeared, sporting the same arrogant manner.

"Good morning, my name is Schmidt, I am responsible for claims. What can I do for you?"

I introduced Suzanna, giving her role in the British ski

team. I repeated my name, policy number, and placed the bill from the Klinik Exzellenz on the table.

Schmidt tapped in the details on a tablet.

"I see...so what is your problem?"

"The problem, Herr Schmidt is the amount of the excess. What you wish me to pay is higher than stipulated in the policy. Contractually, your company is breaking a lawful agreement."

"Presumably, you have not read the entire document," the fellow said, smirking at the thought. "On page eight it clearly states that `in exceptional circumstances, Luzerner Krankenkasse reserves the right to adjust the provision of funds for medical care if the sum exceeds what we believe to be reasonable for the services provided." Schmidt continued, "It`s a standard clause in all our medical policies."

"Wait a minute, your appeal to sportsmen in your advertising, and on page one of the document, it clearly states that Luzerner Krankenkasse will cover all medical charges. When a sportsman is injured, it is the nearest hospital that can best deal with the situation. Athletes travel the world. They cannot be expected to hunt for medical facilities that conform to your financial limitations. There is nothing in your documents, nor in your advertising, to suggest you are specifying certain hospitals whose charges comply with what your company will actually pay." I said evenly, keeping a check on my tone of voice.

"Herr Livesey, you cannot expect us to pay the exorbitant charges some hospitals will charge."

"I do when an injured sportsman needs acute and immediate attention," I replied. "The kind of client you cater for participates in contests around the world, do you think he, or she, is going to check on cheap hospitals before they take to the field, to the water, or, in my case to the snow and ice?"

"Why not? If they want the cover we provide, then that would be a sensible thing to do on their part," answered Schmidt.

"So tell me what is your definition of 'exceptional circumstances'?"

"When we consider the charges submitted to us are too high," he said blithely. "Occasionally, we invoke this clause in our policy."

"As a matter of interest, I have checked the charges for three hospitals in Switzerland, they compare favourably with the Klinik Exzellenz. By the way, have you heard of the EASA?"

"I am not aware what the initials represent, Herr Livesey."

"EASA stands for the European Advertising Standards Alliance, Herr Schmidt. The organisation is based in the Rue des Deux Églises in Brussels. I give you the details because they could well be in touch shortly regarding your misleading medical insurance offer. When the complaint is upheld, I would make sure the International Ski Federation, FIS, publicises the ruling. Moreover, other sports' federations would also be notified."

The smugness on Schmidt's face was fast replaced by a frown as comprehension dawned.

"Let me put this to you," I continued. "No athlete, with one of your medical policies, should be subjected to concern that urgent treatment could be denied because of an insignificant clause hidden in your paperwork. The extra amount you are attempting to make me pay is not a large, it is more what might happen in the future if we sports people suffer serious injury. I would suggest, Herr Schmidt, you review your approach to both the advertising and consider amending the text of your policies. You have my mobile number; I shall hold back submitting the complaint to the EASA for forty-eight hours. Failure to respond during that time and I shall personally deliver it to that authority. Good day to you!"

Once the main door closed behind us, Suzanna let out a deep breath.

"Wow, that told them, Adam," she declared. "I didn't know you were so masterful."

I grinned at her. Then a thought suddenly struck me. "That rough sign on the adjacent office door, I took note of it on the way out. As you said, `UPS` was scribbled on it. Supposing, instead of the parcel delivery company, it stood for the Professional Skiers` Benevolent Fund? In German the fund would translate as `Unterstützungsfond Für Professional Skiläufer`. . .UPS!

"The thing is `UPS` is an organisation many professional skiers subscribe to. Each year we donate for the benefit of skiers who, for whatever reason, have fallen on hard times. As a charity they issue an annual report detailing where the funds are allocated, and I get my copy printed in English. As a result, I have never thought of the Fund's German name," I stroked my chin thoughtfully. "It has always appeared to be a worthy cause, though I doubt many actually take the time to study the paperwork they produce. Come to think of it, I've always posted a cheque to a Post Box reference or given online using my credit card. I knew they were based in Switzerland, but not their actual address. If it's here, in just a room in this building, alongside the Luzerner Krankenkasse, a division of The Insurance Company of Lucerne, I have the strong impression I, and many others, are being taken for a ride."

"Do you think your friend Vasiliev was referring to this `UPS`, and not the delivery service?" Suzanna remarked thoughtfully. "Did he know something, or see someone, that perhaps should not have been there. Possibly they silenced him before he could tell anyone. But, if there were the slight chance he told you, that could be the reason you`re on their hit list."

I stood there, staring at her. Suzanna may well have put her finger on the likely reason for my near misses.

After checking out, Suzanna drove to Montreux, where we stopped for a bite to eat. From there we took Route 9 south, then the switchback road to the Mont Blanc tunnel and on to Tignes. We arrived at the Résidence Bonhomme Neige, the apartment block housing the British team, in the late afternoon.

Somehow, being amongst the team, it did not seem right to share Suzanna`s room, so I booked in again at the Hôtel Le Refuge.

I was unpacking when my mobile rang.

"Hello again." I thought it was Suzanna.

"Herr Livesey?"

It wasn`t. "Speaking."

"Herr Livesey, this is Hans Schmidt of Luzerner Krankenkasse. Herr Livesey, I have spoken at length with the company management, and in the circumstances, we shall be paying all Klinik Exzellenz`s charges, less the normal excess."

"Herr Schmidt, I think you are missing the point. Fine, I do not have to increase the excess payment; but I want Luzerner Krankenkasse to cancel their advertised statement `we will cover all medical charges wherever accidents or injuries occur`. As I said earlier, when a sportsman is injured it is the nearest hospital that can best deal with the situation. Athletes travel the world. They cannot be expected to hunt for medical facilities that conforms to your financial limitations. You are misleading your clients, and they should know clearly what to expect when they seek medical insurance from you."

"I do not think that is possible."

"In which case you leave me no choice. I shall inform the EASA that the company, Luzerner Krankenkasse, is breaking the rules in advertising a non-existent insurance offer. I shall also tell the Swiss Insurance Association, the SIA, that your company is openly switch-selling its policies; and I shall certainly be in touch with the International Ski Federation to warn its members. Doubtless, they will let other athletic bodies know of the situation. I'll give you a further twenty-four hours, Herr Schmidt."

***

"You have not yet completed the task I set you! I do not pay in advance for you to take a leisurely approach to fulfilling my wishes. I want results — otherwise I'll get someone else to do my bidding. If I do, you are aware I never suffer loose ends. For your own safety, I would suggest you make this your number one priority! Do you

understand me?"

"Of course, but you emphasised it should appear an accident. So we tampered with his skis. There is always a risk it will not be a hundred percent successful. That Livesey was hospitalised and recovered was unfortunate, but I won`t let you down."

"You had better not, my friend. . .otherwise."

He did not mention the other attempts to rid the world of Adam Livesey. To propose ill-fortune and the questionable abilities of those he had employed would not be tolerated. From now on he would have to do the deed himself.

CHAPTER EIGHTEEN

From the airport at Adler a coach took us to the ski resort of Rosa Khutor, fifty kilometres north-east of Sochi. Todd had booked the team into the Radisson Hotel. As we approached the town centre, it seemed to me that the buildings, though colourful, still retained that square-built tenement look about them. The shops, though, were more in keeping with western-style facades and interiors.

I was resting on the bed when there was a gentle tap on the door.

When I opened it, Suzanna pushed past me armed with a small travel bag. Unzipping the contents she proceeded to stow them in the bathroom.

"OK. . .strip off. Time for me to apply my potions and lotions, and improve my skills as a masseuse."

The journey had been wearing, and I welcomed her attentions. In fact, her soft hands lulled me to sleep. I awoke with a start when my mobile phone rang.

"Herr Livesey?"

"Speaking."

"It's Herr Schmidt. We shall abide by your request. I shall send an email confirming our intentions."

"Thanks for letting me know, Herr Schmidt. I am

pleased to hear that the required changes are being made."

There was a click. He had disconnected.

"Was that our friend in Lucerne? So they are initiating the changes, that`s good news."

"Not without a little added pressure. Schmidt phoned earlier to tell me that after due consideration I only need pay the normal excess to the Klinik Exzellenz, I told him that was not the point, I wanted revisions to the advertising and to the policies they issue. If not, everyone will hear about their trading methods. That call was to tell me they will make the changes, and they will send me an email to confirm their intentions."

"Well done you! Now go back to sleep for an hour, then get ready for dinner. I`ll come for you at seven thirty, OK?"

I was just finishing in the bathroom when the hotel phone rang.

"Hello?"

"Adam, it`s Alexei. Can I come up?"

A few minutes later there was a tap at the door. I opened it and Alexei strode into the room. I was bare-chested and when he saw the heavy bruising and strapping to my shoulder, remarked. "Wow! it looks like you need a nurse."

A more emphatic knock on the door, and Suzanna arrived.

"I wondered when we might see you, Alexei," she said. "Is everything arranged?"

"It is. We shall collect Adam from the hotel at midday tomorrow."

He turned to me. "The Aeroflot flight leaves at fourteen thirty-five and you will board last and be seated in the first-class section. It gets to Moscow around seventeen thirty. A room is booked for you at the Novotel in Sheremetyevo Airport. The next morning you will take the eleven thirty flight in your own name, and this will get you back to Sochi at fourteen fifteen. A car will be waiting to bring you back to Rosa Khutor. Is that OK with you."

"Yes, but what name shall I be using on the flight to Moscow?"

"Alexei Sokolov. Here's my passport," said Alexei. "We are roughly the same height and colouring. In any case, you will not be stopped. If you were, just wave the passport. There's a government stamp in it, as a consequence, no one will query what you are up to or where you're going."

"So there's no need to collect him from Sochi Airport?" Suzanna asked.

"No, all that is taken care of," Alexei replied. "Look, Adam, I really appreciate what you are doing. There was no one else I could turn to. I would certainly not have dared ask a Russian."

He reached out and shook my hand.

"That's what friends are for, Alexei," I said quietly. "I know you would do the same for me if it were necessary."

He clasped my hand again. His eyes were moist.

"I must go," he muttered. "See you tomorrow."

The door slowly closed behind him.

I turned to see Suzanna biting her lip. "What?"

"Supposing you get caught. Supposing his little scheme doesn't work, you might not be able to leave

Russia. Now I`m starting to get worried," she sniffed.

"Come here," I put my arms around her. "Nothing can go wrong. Don`t get concerned, darling."

I quickly dressed, and we went down for dinner.

CHAPTER NINETEEN

He was punctual almost to the minute.

The ambulance drew up, the rear doors opened, and I was helped into its interior.

Three-quarters of an hour later we drew up outside the terminal building. I was pushed down the vehicle ramp in a wheelchair by my accompanying nurse as a female attendant hurried to greet us.

The VIP Lounge is separate from the regular passenger section, and the attendant steered me through its tall glass doors to a reception desk. I was aware of the sympathetic glances of another attendant while she registered the flight details. My damaged shoulder had been lightly plastered to appear a broken collar bone; and a tight dressing applied to my chest held me stiffly upright; but the most uncomfortable part of the whole procedure was the splint behind my left knee, which allowed for only limited movement of the joint.

What I did find disconcerting was what had been done to my face. In the ambulance a woman had used cosmetics skilfully to suggest severe cuts and bruises. After which she had given me spectacles to wear. I had not been allowed to look in a mirror; but when I was wheeled into the seating area, I received numerous glances from other passengers.

Eventually, the flight was called, and the nurse, accompanied by yet another attendant, pushed through the departure lounge down the jetway to the plane door. I was helped from the wheelchair and supported to my first-row seat. My female nurse sat in the aisle seat, and frequently asked if I were OK, could she provide anything.

And so nearly three hours passed in a series of uncomfortable positions. Turning my body this way and that without finding any respite from the painful dressings attached to me.

Eventually, the plane landed in Moscow; and while we sat there, passengers started making their way forward towards the exit.

"I thought it was you, Alexei," said a tall, full-figured individual in his fifties. Ignoring the nurse he leaned over her head. "Well, well, you`ve come unstuck this time with your free-riding on the slopes. You`ll be out of the picture for a while, I shouldn`t wonder. I`ll wager your boss will have something to say about that."

The fellow, laughing at his remark, was preparing to continue his taunts, until urged to move off the plane by those behind him. I had only understood snatches of what he said, but it was enough to realise he was delighting in Alexei`s supposed misfortune. A good thing he had not peered too closely and seen through my disguise.

When the plane had finally emptied, our carry-on bags were retrieved from the overhead locker and my wheelchair from the baggage hold. The nurse pushed me through the terminal to a waiting minibus. I was helped into a seat, and the chair stowed in the rear.

We were driven round to the Novotel, chosen principally for the continuous stream of people arriving and departing at all hours; thus, their constant demand for attention at both the reception and the concierge's desks meant we received only the briefest of attention.

The nurse signed the register and paid for a night's accommodation. We took the lift to the third floor, and she wheeled me along the carpeted corridor to our room.

Opening the door Olga Petrova, the nurse, pushed me to the centre of the room, and sat back heavily on the bed.

"Thank you Mr Livesey," she said in heavily-accented English. "You returned me to Moscow without anyone knowing."

"Not at all, Miss Petrova. Though I was worried when that fellow on the plane thought I was Alexei."

"So was I, for that was Adrik Turgenev, a journalist who works for Moscow's daily tabloid, Komsomolskaya Pravda. I was just a nurse to whom he need pay little attention. If he had recognised me, it would have been all over tomorrow's front page."

She laughed. "To think I was actually sitting under his very nose. That will amuse Leoni."

"But how did he know Alexei Sokolov was on the plane?" I queried.

"Mr Livesey, whenever they are travelling, people like him bribe airline staff for sight of the manifests. If someone of importance is on the same flight, that could well lead to a key interview, or the off-chance they have something to hide," she grinned. "Like me, for example."

I went to get up from the wheelchair.

"Wait, before we go any further, let me help you out of your various dressings and clear the bruising and scars from your face."

"First Miss Petrova, I want to look in the mirror in the bathroom. Any number of people have shown sadness at the damage to my face."

I turned on the light, and stood back in horror. It dawned on me that people`s stares could have been more of pity than concern.

"Can you clean my face before anything else?" I requested. "It looks like I`ve been in a car accident rather than a fall when skiing."

From one of the carry-on bags she withdrew various bottles, and using their contents on cotton wool, began wiping my face. Gradually features appeared that I recognised.

We took a taxi to the Oblomov Restaurant on Monetchikovskiy Pereulok. This was the second phase of Sokolov`s plan. Choose an up-market restaurant to make sure Olga Petrova is seen and acknowledged by Moscow`s glitterati.

That evening our roles were reversed. I was there as her silent escort. During the meal a number of people stopped by, their interest fixed solely on Olga. I got on with my meal, barely aware of the bright conversations taking place the other side of the table.

We were late leaving the restaurant. Someone had called a taxi for us, which drove across the city to her high-rise apartment on Krasnogvardeyskiy proezd.

"Thank you for a delightful evening, Adam. I think it worked, don`t you?"

"From what little I understood, Olga, you very firmly established that you were here, in Moscow with those that mattered."

She leaned forward and kissed my cheek.

"Remember me, Adam. We shall probably never meet again."

With that she opened the taxi door and walked towards the apartment block.

It was a short ride north to Sheremetyevo Airport and the Novotel.

That night I hid the wheelchair in a service cupboard along the corridor. The next morning I took the courtesy bus round to the terminal, and enjoyed a comfortable, first class seat and service on the flight to Sochi.

CHAPTER TWENTY

I had spoken with Suzanna on two occasions. When we arrived in Moscow, to wish her goodnight, and on the return flight to Sochi. To our relief I confirmed all had gone to plan.

Halfway through the flight, Sokolov called me.

"All is well, Alexei I`m on the plane back to Sochi."

"I know, old friend. I spoke with Olga this morning. You did a terrific job. She told me about your brush with Adrik Turgenev, that was a close call."

"Olga was highly amused that he ignored her, even when she was sitting right under his nose," I said, smiling at the thought.

"Perhaps we can have dinner together, Suzanna, you and I?" Sokolov suggested. "We have something to celebrate, and the treat is on me. I`ll pick you up from the Radisson at seven thirty this evening, is that OK?"

"We shall look forward to it. This afternoon I`ll be on the slopes cheering on our skiers. By the time we get back to the hotel I`ll be frozen, so can you choose a restaurant which has the central heating on at full blast?"

After the airline snack I closed my eyes and my thoughts turned, yet again, to Suzanna. It certainly was a whirlwind romance, and developing at such a hectic pace I wondered if it would burn itself out. Would I be greatly upset?

I refused to answer my own question.

Instead, I cast my mind back to my younger days. I was never given to pangs of the lovelorn. I had girlfriends, but they seemed to come and go without the heartbreak suffered by others. Invariably I loved the current enchantress; but when she found another, we parted without rancour. The world did not come close to an end.

Although, I clearly remember our household was frequently rent with the emotional upheavals of my siblings. They appeared to move from one `light of their life` to the next in a seesaw of passionate highs and lows.

I, on the other hand, sailed through this phase of my formative years with emotions comfortably undisturbed. At university, liaisons lasted longer. Penelope and I were together for almost eighteen months. She was attractive, lively-minded and not too demanding. I never thought about the future. Penny was there: the unstated presumption was she would be there tomorrow and, no doubt, the day after.

She was a year ahead of me. Suddenly she graduated, took her electric kettle, and kissed me goodbye. I was a little put out, but not distraught. Others came into my life leaving the same untroubled impression.

But now passions, rarely inflamed, were hard to control. In the brief moments Suzanna and I were apart, this need to analyse what was happening to me dominated my every thought. I tried to untangle feelings, to think rationally; but she was the constant throughout all my waking hours. Never before had I been so emotionally overwhelmed — and jealous when other men briefly commanded her attention. This was a brand new emotion. Perhaps, I ought to stand back from this burgeoning relationship. Create space, take a more objective view of the affair.

When the taxi pulled up outside the Radisson, Suzanna rushed out to greet me. There was a moment of coming gently together. She, trying to gauge how firmly to grip my undamaged parts; I, steeling myself against the strength of the embrace she would exert. But we managed; and in that moment all my profound intentions came to nothing.

    I realised I shall probably still have disconcerting thoughts about our future; yet they seemed to evaporate whenever in her presence.

CHAPTER TWENTY-ONE

Dinner was at a restaurant called the Red Fox. A large timber structure of beams, panelling and tables of thick irregular planks. Soft lighting and the smell of cedar added to the atmosphere, and it was pleasantly warm.

Suzanna was enchanted. "What a delightful place, Alexei. If the food is as good as the décor we are in for a treat."

It was. And as the wine mellowed our senses, as a consequence, Alexei was more open in his conversation. I remembered how he became maudlin on the occasion we had dinner together in Vienna; and wondered if I would be picking up the bill, as I did on that occasion.

We had consumed several bottles of wine, when Alexei raised his glass, and mumbled, "*За моего хорошего друга Анатолия Васильева, пусть он прыгает на небесах!*"

Suzanna stared at him. "Did you know Anatoly Vasiliev?"

"I didn`t know you understood Russian, Suzanna." I had only caught a fraction of Alexei`s remark, but I certainly picked up Anatoly`s name. "What did Alexei say?"

"Something like, `Here's to you, Anatoly Vasiliev, may you be ski jumping in heaven.'"

We both turned in his direction.

"Yes, he was a good friend. We both lived in the same apartment building in Moscow," he added.

"He was also close to Adam," Suzanna declared. "In fact, he was there, at Bischofshofen, when the accident occurred."

Sokolov was suddenly keen to hear exactly what I had seen when Vasiliev jumped to his death.

"I was watching from the side of the runout. The leap off the ramp was text-book. He leaned into the flight, and assumed the ideal outward pointing of his skis. However, at that moment, the binding on his left ski was actuated. The ski fell away, and as it did so, his aeronautical stance turned into a nightmare crash landing. I clambered over the barrier and ran towards him. The paramedics were first on the scene, but there was little they could do. Anatoly briefly opened his eyes, saw me, and whispered two words: `microswitch` and `UPS`.

"What `UPS` as in the `United Parcel Service`?"

"It is a possibility. . .but we have also just realised that `UPS` could be the initials of `Unterstützungsfond Für Professional Skiläufer`. It's an organisation most professional skiers make donations to. I've never known where they actually operate. . . until Suzanna and I walked past their likely office in Lucerne."

"There is the strong possibility," Suzanna remarked, "that when Anatoly was in Lucerne he happened to learn, or see someone who should not have been there. Moreover, I am now convinced that whoever they are believes he may have told Adam, which could be the reason he appears to be on their hit list."

"Thinking about the accident," I continued. "I should have examined Anatoly's skis. I went with him to the hospital, and missed the opportunity."

"All is not lost, my friend," Alexei declared. "I have photos of both his skis. I got them from the pathologist's office some days afterwards," Sokolov commented. "Apparently, he is not a skier and couldn't tell anything as to cause. He simply reported the incident as 'accidental death'."

He stopped, deep in thought for a moment. "Actually, I've got the photos with me at the President's place. Perhaps, I could bring them over tomorrow afternoon and show them to you. You can tell me what you think."

"OK, but make it late afternoon, Suzanna is skiing tomorrow," I said.

"Right, I'll be with you about four o'clock."

I watched from the runout as Suzanna came a very creditable fifth in the Women's Super G. In fact, there was no more than four tenths of a second between her and first place.

When she joined Todd, myself and the others, her delight was palpable.

"What did you think, Adam?" she said excitedly. "Do you think I can go any faster."

Before I could reply, Lars Oestennson appeared by her side. "I'm sure of it. I'll help if you like?"

Why do I let that guy get under my skin, I wondered. Probably because he is always trying to muscle in, even though everyone else regards us as a couple. Suzanna keeps him at arm's length, but at the same time she seems to delight in his attentions. Is it to make me jealous?

Possibly, to keep me on my toes. Well, Miss Bancroft, two can play at that game.

The opportunity came quicker than I imagined.

Angela and Lisa were both skiing in the Women`s Slalom. Lisa looked particularly able, skiing with a stylish grace as she swept through the gates.

Suzanna was in discussion with Todd, so after the girls had finished, I went back to the hotel with them. Lisa was limping slightly when we entered Todd`s suite, which we were all using as the team members` common room.

As she dropped into a chair Lisa cried out, "Ouch, I`ve got cramp in my legs."

I walked quickly over to her, lifted her legs, and began pushing her toes back and heels forward in the classic method of easing the discomfort.

"Thanks, Adam," she said gritting her teeth. "Now I`ve got spasms in my right calf."

I was massaging Lisa`s leg when the door opened and Suzanna walked in. It took her a second to get the wrong end of the stick; turning on her heel she marched out slamming the door behind her.

"Oh, oh. . .have I caused a problem?" Lisa murmured.

"Of course not. It was all perfectly innocent," I replied. "I`ll go and tell her what I was doing."

"She could see what you were doing," grinned Angela.

I went along the corridor to our room.

As I entered a vase hit the door and broke into pieces.

"I`m a shy kind of person, he said. Well, you didn`t look shy just now, stroking her legs. So that`s how you entice women into your bed, is it? Acting the coy, reserved type. I should have known better, idiot that I am to fall for someone like you."

She sniffed. "Well, I can't stay in here any longer. I'll bed down somewhere else."

She stood up from the bed, and I grabbed her arms, pinning them to her sides. "For your information, I was not making advances on Lisa. She had cramp in both legs, and I held onto her feet. When she developed spasms in her right calf I was attempting to ease the pain and the problem."

"A good story!"

"Angela was there, she'll tell you what happened."

"I didn't see her," Suzanna said, uncertainty in her voice.

"Well she was. You weren't looking at anyone else except me, supposedly making advances."

"Is it true, you were just being helpful?"

"Yes."

"Oh God, what am I going to say to them? Sorry, I jumped to the wrong conclusion? But you were rubbing Lisa's legs," she sniffed again, "when you should be rubbing mine."

Suzanna eased her arms from my grip, and put them round my neck pulling me tight to her.

I whispered in her ear. "I do believe you were jealous."

"When I catch you fondling someone else I have every right to be."

"Now you know how I feel about Lars Oestensson. I don't like him putting his arm around you, whispering in your ear, as I'm doing now, and trying to tempt you away from me. Now you know how it feels."

Sokolov joined Suzanna and I at the table in Todd's suite.

After congratulating Suzanna on her run, he opened a briefcase and drew out a brown A4 envelope. From the opening tumbled a dozen colour photographs. He searched a little more and brought out a magnifying glass. He then proceeded to lay out each of the photographs, four of which were trained on the left binding.

I had seen the TV pictures showing the moment the ski and Anatoly parted company. They portrayed the metal bar at the heel coming loose, but the safety cord should have retained it. Then the left binding released and the ski fell away.

My attention was immediately drawn to the height bar at the heel of the binding. To allow jumpers to soar at the desired angle of both body and skis, the heels of the ski boots can be raised. By how much is a personal choice. Tabs lock into the jumper's boots, and ride up the bar, but not beyond a determined level. If anything were to go wrong with either bar, a cord, tied between the ski platform and boot lock, acts as a failsafe mechanism to prevent the ski from going beyond the selected height.

I reached for the magnifying glass, and peered intently at one particular picture. It clearly showed a fractured height bar and the remnants of the safety cord.

"Have a look at this, Suzanna," I said, over my shoulder.

She spent several minutes studying the detail of the binding.

When she straightened up, I could see from her face that she had come to the same conclusion.

"Alexei, I think Suzanna and I are in agreement. These photographs clearly show the left ski was sabotaged. As Anatoly leapt from the ramp the downward force of his body, giving him added impetus, was enough to shear the height bar which had been tampered with, and the partly-severed safety cord would have snapped at the slightest pressure. It was inevitable the binding would release and he would tumble to his death."

"Боже правый! Who would do such a thing?" Sokolov muttered angrily.

"As Suzanna and I said earlier, the only conclusion we can draw, Alexei," I murmured, "is when Anatoly was in Lucerne, he saw something or someone he shouldn`t have done. . . and they killed him for being in the wrong place at the wrong time."

"I should add, Alexei," said Suzanna, "we now realise that the accidents and near misses he has recently encountered were deliberate. This last attempt almost succeeded. It put him in hospital. At first, it was touch and go."

"What are you saying Suzanna? Adam`s life is in danger as well?"

"Quite possibly. We think it`s because whoever are behind it believes Anatoly told Adam what he saw."

"And all he managed to say was, `microswitch` and `UPS`," I added.

"That`s right," murmured Suzanna.

"Let me get this straight," Alexei remarked "Are you saying the car crash Adam witnessed was really intended for him? And the skiing accident he suffered was a genuine attempt on his life?"

"Without a doubt," said Suzanna. "Where the car crash was concerned, they hit the wrong car. Adam had changed vehicles for a larger one, and they, whomever they are, made the mistake of smashing into a car similar to the one he had previously been driving."

"And the skiing accident?"

"Unbeknown to me, the binding was adjusted to light pressure," I explained. "So when I landed heavily after the last jump, the binding released the ski and I careered off the course, winding up in hospital."

"How on earth could anyone be so callous!" murmured Sokolov. "Do you know who did it?"

"It was the technician who prepared the skis for me, a fellow called Ron Grainger," I said ruefully. "Suzanna found the ski he had tampered with in one of the hotel`s refuse skips. A search was made, but, by then, he had disappeared."

"So what is to stop them trying again? What sort of protection have you set up?" Alexei queried.

Well. . . none really. It has only just sunk in," I replied.

Alexei stared hard at me. "You realise, of course, that if they think you`ve told Suzanna, she, too, becomes a target. Look, I may be able to help. I have a contact; I could organise some sort of protection."

I glanced at Suzanna. "What do you think?"

"As I see it, Alexei, if Anatoly had told Adam what he saw, he would most certainly have involved the authorities after these attempts to silence him. The fact that he hasn`t must surely indicate he knows nothing, that Anatoly didn`t pass on anything to him."

"I hadn`t considered that aspect," I added. "We should be all right from now on. But thanks Alexei for the offer."

"Listen, my friends, don`t accept the logic you apply to yourselves as the guiding light for others. It may have gone too far."

"What do you mean by that?" Suzanna queried.

"Simply this, having failed thus far, you could now be their enduring quarry. They may now regard you as persistent targets. Whatever the original cause is now forgotten. You have to be eliminated for no other reason than you are still alive."

"That`s too morbid even to contemplate, Alexei," said Suzanna. "I just can`t believe that to be true."

CHAPTER TWENTY-TWO

"Todd, I want to ski the Super G at Aspen."

"Are you out of your tidy mind! You could hardly walk at Rosa Khutor! You`re not skiing in Aspen!"

We were on the way back to Tignes. On the Aeroflot flight to Milan, I had been deep in thought. With the GB Championships coming up, I had to get back on skis before then, and experience some hard competition.

When we boarded the coach for the four-hour journey to the British team`s training camp, I made a point of sitting close to the performance director. Even Suzanna did not know what I had in mind. That is, until he raised his voice.

"Did I hear Todd correctly? What on earth are you thinking?" she exclaimed.

"I need to get back on skis. I thought if I competed in the Super G at Aspen it would set me up for the British Championships. I wouldn`t drive myself, but I need to see how much I can do, and whether I shall be race fit in time for our home tournament."

"No!"

"What do you mean, no?" It`s my body. . . it`s up to me when I put on skis."

"If you ski against all the advice you've been given, you're on your own, Adam. You're being reckless, and I don't want to know someone who deliberately puts his wellbeing on the line! Excuse me."

She eased herself past me and took a seat at the rear of the coach.

Our first argument. . .and judging by her parting words, possibly the last.

In a way she was right; but I could not allow her to make decisions for me. That would make for the wrong kind of relationship. It made me even more determined to ski the Super G.

I took a room at the Résidence Bonhomme Neige, the team's headquarters. But Suzanna did not join me. Nor did she come to dinner.

In fact, we avoided each other, even when the team flew to Aspen. The plane from Turin landed in Denver, and we boarded a local flight to Aspen's Pitkin County Airport.

A coach collected us and all our equipment and drove the six miles to Snowmass Village, where the championships were taking place. We were booked into the Stonebridge Inn, not far from the gondola station.

The Super G, for both men and women, was scheduled to be held on the Friday, in four days' time. This was beneficial for me; I could ski each day and gradually accustom my body to the demands of the race. There is little else one can do in preparation. Being a single run event, skiers are only confronted with the course shortly before the race.

Taking myself off to the gentle slopes, away from the crowds and competitors, I started slowly to get into skiing mode. It was painful initially, then a dull ache, to just being uncomfortable. But I persisted.

At mealtimes, wherever I sat at a table, Suzanna always seemed to be some distance from me. I was fast coming to the conclusion our relationship was over. It had burnt itself out. Like a Roman candle firework, I thought, lots of sparkle, stars shooting out, then dying, leaving just the shattered husk. The trouble was I missed her terribly. She may be able to shrug it off, but I had come to realise that life without her was an unwelcome prospect.

***

"You have disappointed me. Are you losing your touch, I wonder? No more excuses, this time make it happen. . .in fact, completing the task in the United States will be better. There will be less likelihood of any comeback."

"But you have always insisted it should appear an accident. . ."

"Forget that, just do it!"

CHAPTER TWENTY-THREE

Race day.

I managed to ski alongside the course, speaking into my pocket voice recorder, I took note of the steeper parts of the slope, the turns, those with an adverse camber, and the positioning of the thirty gates.

The women's Super G was first. I had to watch and cheer on Suzanna, even if she was not aware of my presence at the barrier. She is a strong skier, almost fearless the manner in which she comes down the course. Tight on the gates, good body lean as she tackles the jumps and always has a powerful finish.

As she burst across the finishing line and executed a parallel stop, Suzanna's helmeted head turned, scanning the crowd. I'm sure she saw me clapping, a broad smile on my face, before she made her way to the exit.

What is more she posted the third fastest time, a wonderful achievement.

Then it was the men's turn.

In the field of twenty-five I was drawn in nineteenth place.

In the company of several other skiers in the gondola, I made my way up to the start. As competitors were called forward, so numbers thinned and soon it was the moment to join others in the starting hut. In there I have always found the atmosphere changes sharply. Standing in a short line, those in front of you are rehearsing their path down the mountain, leaning this way and that as they mentally picture the run.

I had no illusions that my effort today would challenge the top skiers.

I would do my damnedest, but I was tuning up, mentally and physically, for what lay ahead.

"Livesey, number nineteen!"

The moment had arrived.

I shuffled forward, poles over the starting wand.

The countdown. . . and then I was off. The exhilaration of the start was soon swept away as I came quickly upon the first gate. Leaning into the turn, a sharp twinge made me gasp. Straightening up I headed for the next.

I had not expected my breathing to affect me, but as I slipped through the next few gates I started to pant, which caused first discomfort then increasing torment in my chest.

Perhaps, because I was not committed fully, straining every sinew to ski faster, I did not suffer the fate of seven racers who missed gates or crashed out the course. The slope is a challenge. A twisting course with numerous bumps to catch the unwary.

Halfway down I was wracked with pain. So much so, my vision was blurring, and my legs were stiffening up from the damage caused by the accident.

I had underestimated my ability to ski through the

discomfort. One last turn and the final gate. Thank god it was a straight run to the finish.

I managed one last effort to come to a halt in the runout. Now at a standstill I slowly toppled over and was losing consciousness when I felt my helmet being removed and cool hands holding my head.

"You, stupid, stupid man," Suzanna cried. Tears splashed my face, yet my heart leapt.

"Suzanna, you were right. . .I am stupid. . .about you."

I received a wet, tearful kiss. "Don`t, please, try to be superhuman. At least when you are injured."

Suddenly, other hands lifted me up and I managed, with Suzanna`s help, to make it to the exit, eventually back to the Stonebridge, and to my room.

I lay on the bed. I felt weak, my limbs unresponsive.

"Suzanna, by the slightest chance, do you have any of your magic potions with you?"

She came over to me. "Of course, knowing what you might do, I brought them with me." She stared at me intently, then said. "Does your face hurt?"

"The rest of me does, but not my face."

"Good!"

Then she kissed me. Gently, then with increasing passion. I could hardly breathe.

When we parted I said. "Tomorrow`s headlines. The skier, though severely injured, did not die from his wounds, but from asphyxiation."

She hit me with a pillow.

"I`ll go and get them."

After half an hour I began to wonder if she were coming back.

Suddenly, the door opened and Suzanna appeared, trailing two suitcases.

"If I'm going to nurse you, I have to be close to the patient," she said with a knowing grin.

It was while she was massaging my chest, I asked the question.

"By the way do you know how the race went? Who won?"

"An Italian, I can't remember his name. He did it in one minute, eight point two five seconds. I remembered your time, one minute ten point four seconds. You came eighteenth. Not bad for one of the walking-wounded."

"By the way what time is the award ceremony? I don't want to miss that."

"Six o'clock. . .plenty of time. Right, move over."

She snuggled up to me, the best cure I know for my injuries. Once more, I was a truly contented man.

Suzanna was the brightest star of the British competitors.

Although everyone put in good performances, she was the only one to make the podium and receive a trophy and more FIS points. Predictably, I clapped and cheered the loudest.

Although my aches and pains had largely subsided to a dull ache, combatting it was tiring. As a consequence, I left Suzanna with the other team members and went to my room early. I had only the faintest recollection of her slipping beneath the duvet later.

I was feeling much better the following morning, and we joined others in the breakfast room. I was surprised to see Lars Oestensson sitting next to Lisa. During a conversation with her, she asked me. "Are you coming to the party in Aspen tonight, Adam?"

"What party's that?"

Suzanna took up the conversation. "I haven't mentioned it to Adam yet, Lisa. I wanted to see how he felt this morning, and whether he'd be up to it."

"So what party is it?" I asked again.

We were talking to some of the American team last night, and got invited to a crud party at the Jerome Hotel in Aspen," Lisa said.

"Crud party? What on earth is that?" I queried.

"Let me call one of them over, and he can explain." She jumped up and crossed to a nearby table. After a moment she returned with a skier I had last seen in the starting hut the previous day.

Lisa introduced him. "Reece, this is Adam. Adam, Reece."

He stood there for a moment staring at me. "I've seen you before somewhere, Adam. Now, where would that have been?" he said, stroking his chin.

I grinned. "Lining up in the starting hut."

"That's right." He leaned over the table and shook my hand.

"So you want to know what a crud party is. Well, I guess you've asked the right guy. I'm an Aspen boy through and through. Lived here all my life."

"Sit down, Reece, you'll be more comfortable," Lisa patted the seat next to her.

He nodded and lowered himself onto the chair, and leaned forward with his elbows on the table.

"The J-Bar, part of the Jerome Hotel on Main Street, has been the social hub of the town since miners came to Aspen during the days of the silver boom. When Prohibition struck in 1920, the J-Bar went the way of a host of other bars across America: it became a soda fountain. Necessity is the mother of invention, they say, and it wasn`t long before those in the know learned to circumvent the alcohol ban by ordering bourbon-spiked vanilla milkshakes.

"What to call it without giving the game away. Simple, give it a derogatory term, and so the `crud` was born. The infamous Aspen Crud still lives on today, made with hotel's freshly churned vanilla ice cream infused with bourbon.

"We regularly celebrate the advent of the drink with a party. If you`re up for it, join us this evening, you`d be more than welcome."

"I`ve booked a hair appointment in Aspen at two thirty. Will you come with me? We can get a taxi into the town."

"Sure. . .do you know where it is?"

"According to the receptionist Aspen Hair is on East Hyman Avenue. I also want to buy some postcards to send to my nieces and nephews. I always send cards wherever I am away skiing or holidaying."

"That`s a nice idea. While I`m waiting I can buy them for you? How many shall I buy?"

Suzanna did a quick mental calculation.

"Seven, no make it eight. One of my sisters` children is coming up to seven, so she`ll want one now."

"How many sisters or brothers do you have?" I asked.

"No boys, three sisters, I`m the youngest. What about you?"

"I have two sisters and a brother. Evelyn, Frieda and Lukas. My mother is Austrian, so my parents decided they would alternate between British and Austrian names. They are all married, and have children."

"I'd love to meet them," Suzanna remarked.

"They all live in and around Oxford. If you like, we could stop off in England for a few days on our way back to Tignes. What do you think?"

"That would be great. But hadn't you better check with your parents first?"

"I'll give them a ring. But it won't be a problem."

I left Suzanna at the hairdressers, and wandered along the pedestrian shopping mall, stopping here and there to peer into windows. I bought twelve cards and stamps, and eventually took a seat in a coffee shop, more to escape the cold.

Lost in thought, I was looking out at the passers-by, when suddenly my eyes alighted on a figure hurrying along the mall. It was Josh Finden...or was it? Wrapped up against the chill wind I had no clear sight of his face; but the way the person walked and his height matched the man who was my agent.

If it were Josh, that was odd, he had mentioned he was not coming to Aspen, but meeting potential clients in Vienna. He had many strings to his bow. I knew his interests covered a number of sports.

I must have been mistaken.

Later, when I met Suzanna, I mentioned the possible sighting. But she thought I had made a mistake. "I remember him saying quite clearly he was going to Vienna," she added.

Two taxis took eight of us, including Lars Oestensson, to the crud party in Aspen.

In the J-Bar we were met by Reece — `glad you could make it` — and ushered towards the bar. Leaning over, he called. "Hey, Jeanie, crud for my British friends!"

"Coming up, Reece."

The salon was packed, and the noise of conversation almost deafening.

Reece, started handing round the glasses.

"Normally, we drink it out of tin mugs as they did in Prohibition times," Reece said loudly. "So what do you think?"

I took a careful sip.

"Not like that, Adam. A good mouthful," he grinned.

So I did, encountering first the benign taste of the milkshake, then the kick from the alcohol. It caught my breath for a moment.

"Wow, it creeps up on you," I gasped with watery eyes. "What`s in this?"

"Well, the main ones are French vanilla ice cream and three shots of bourbon. Have another."

It was close to ten o`clock when Suzanna took a closer look at me.

"You`re in pain, aren`t you?"

"Not exactly, more uncomfortable."

We had been standing for two hours and now I was flagging.

"I`ll find Reece, thank him, and tell him you and I are leaving."

Outside the hotel we started walking west on Main Street, looking for a cab. We were close to the offices of the Aspen Times, when the lights in the newspaper building shone on a tall figure stepping out of the shadows. The hat he was wearing had a wide brim obscuring his features. His stiff right arm was holding a gun, and it was pointed directly at us.

It seemed to take forever as I moved in front of Suzanna. My first thoughts were we're about to be mugged. But not a word had been spoken. The gunman edged a little to his right. I could see him tense to pull the trigger. This is it I thought, they've finally caught up with me.

Two shots rang out.

I waited for my life to expire but our would-be assassin was still pointing his firearm at me. Then slowly his arm sank, and he toppled over onto the sidewalk.

I turned to see our saviour, and into the half-light strode Josh Finden.

"My God, am I glad to see you," I exclaimed. "Did you fire that shot?"

"Yes, just a fraction of a second before he fired at me." Josh nodded towards the body. "Now, don't hang around, move on quickly. I'll sort out your likely killer. Move! And get out of Aspen as soon as you can."

"Right." I turned to thank him again, and saw a shadowy figure standing just behind Josh Finden.

I can't remember making our way back to the Stonebridge Inn.

When the cab dropped Suzanna and I at the entrance, she was still shaking when I helped her out the vehicle.

That night we clung together for mutual comfort; and it was only when we had boarded the plane for Chicago the next day that I let out a sigh of relief.

"It`s behind now, Suzanna." I said, taking hold of her hand.

In fact, although badly shaken last night, she appeared to have recovered more quickly than I.

"When that gun was pointing straight at us, I thought someone was playing a bad joke," she said in a low voice. "I had had too many glasses of their crud to believe it was for real. But when those shots rang out, I was instantly sober, and very afraid. God knows what happened afterwards. . . and I don`t want to know."

She squeezed my hand tightly.

My thoughts centred on what Josh Finden was doing in Aspen? How did he come to be on Main Street at ten o`clock on a Saturday night. . .and why was he carrying a gun?"

CHAPTER TWENTY-FOUR

We waited two hours for the connecting flight from O'Hare Airport in Chicago to London Heathrow. While we were in the departure lounge I phoned my mother in Oxford.

Her first words were, "You didn't put up much of a show in the Super G in Aspen, dear. Did something go wrong?"

"Unfortunately, I was still suffering from the crash in St. Moritz. But things are gradually improving. Look, Mother, we, Suzanna and I, are about to board a plane to Heathrow. Would it be convenient to come up to Oxford for a few days?"

"Of course, you know you're always welcome. When will you be arriving?"

"With the time difference, we'll be landing about nine tomorrow morning. I'll hire a car, so we could be with you about eleven o'clock. Is that OK?"

"Fine, I'll mention it to Evelyn. I know she'd like to see you."

I closed the call, and turned to Suzanna.

"Well, I did as you suggested, now mother is going to tell my sister Evelyn."

"What`s wrong with that?"

"Evelyn, my dear young lady, is the family gossip. More than likely she will tell my other sister and brother, and our arrival will turn into a Livesey family gathering."

"Well, I for one, would enjoy that. I really would like to meet all your family."

I shook my head. "You don`t know what you`re asking."

An uneventful flight. . .just how I like it.

We cleared immigration; our luggage appeared on the carousel; and our skis arrived a short while after. Only a few people were at the Hertz desk, and by ten o`clock we were on the road heading for the M40 motorway.

Suzanna was quiet for much of the journey; but as we approached Oxford from the north, avoiding the traffic in the city, she said quietly. "Adam, I don`t think we should mention last night`s incident, do you? We wouldn`t want to alarm anybody."

I pondered on her comment.

"I think you`re probably right. My mother already believes that someone is out to get me. She`d have proof if we told her. Especially, my agent shooting our would-be assassin. I wonder what he did with the body?"

She shuddered. "I don`t want to think about it. I`ve come to terms with what happened, and who our rescuer was. If he disposed of it some way, Josh must have had help. So what was he and whoever is his assistant, doing outside the Jerome Hotel at ten o`clock at night?"

"I had similar thoughts on the plane," I murmured. "Not only that, he had a gun with him. So, was he expecting trouble?"

"When are you next seeing him?"

"Obviously, I'm in frequent touch with him. But the questions to which we need answers would be best put face-to-face, not in an email or text message. However, he will certainly be at the British Championships in Tignes in a fortnight's time."

"You know I'm competing in the women's Super G in Bormio next week," Suzanna reminded me. She was quiet for a moment before adding. "I think it would be best if I go with members of the team. You can then spend time in Tignes. There's safety in numbers, and you can gently prepare for the Championships."

"You're right. I need to tune up for the Downhill with a few runs on the slopes."

I turned in through the gates of my parents' Edwardian, red-brick house, and heard Suzanna say, "Fascinating, there's a hint of the gothic about your home, Adam. I like it."

Having been reared from a small child within its walls, I had never considered it to be other than, well, home. It was not until she made that remark that I re-appraised the house with a different eye. To my mind it had character, though not necessarily great charm. But it was where I had spent all my formative years, and it still beckoned as my sanctuary.

"They're here!" I heard someone shout. The front door opened, and we were besieged by an army of parents, siblings and their offspring.

"I'm so pleased to meet you, Suzanna," declared my mother. "I hear you have been Adam's nurse, adviser, and close friend since you met. I hope you have managed to keep him in check, we never could. Even as a boy he was headstrong."

"Not quite yet, Mrs Livesey," grinned Suzanna.

"Call me Annika, my dear," said my mother. "Now let me introduce you to everyone. But first, let`s all go into the conservatory. We don`t want to get too cold standing out here."

We dutifully trooped through the house to a broad expanse of glass, housing oversize plants, comfortable chairs and sofas.

"What a magnificent conservatory," declared Suzanna, "it`s so warm and welcoming."

"Yes, we like it. You can sit in here in the depths of winter and it will still feel warm and cosy. Anyway, sit yourselves down and we`ll have some tea. You do drink tea, do you Suzanna?"

"Yes, thank you, Annika." she replied. "But could I have it black, and no sugar?"

"Of course, my dear. Now let me quickly run through who we all are. You won`t remember everyone straight away, but it doesn`t matter. I`ll point out each member of the Livesey clan, and give their names."

My mother quickly identified those present, and then disappeared into the kitchen with my sister, Evelyn.

Suzanna was busy talking with my father and Lukas, and I sat there idly looking at them across the conservatory in conversation. I felt a hand on my arm. "She`s just what you need, little brother," murmured Frieda. "I have the impression she has a will of her own, and won`t be dictated to. Am I right?"

"So I have discovered. She also speaks her mind. . .no beating about the bush."

"Good, I like her, Adam," she added, in a low voice.

What surprised me, Suzanna even remembered the names of all the children. Even now I'm hard-pressed to recall them, and have to be reminded of their birthdays.

We stayed for two days, during which time I showed her around the city. Father was clearly taken with her: even to the extent of giving her a guided tour of St. Anne's College, and readily remembering her name. There was no hesitation. Unlike the slight pause he invariably adopts with me when bringing to mind the name of his youngest son.

Mother clearly hit it off with Suzanna. On much of the journey back to Heathrow, she commented about the serene way she organised the household, dealt with the family, and had such an engaging personality.

"I can well see why your father wasted little time in pursuing her and asking her to marry him," she said.

"Knowing my mother," I blithely remarked. "I can tell you she probably planned their meeting, engagement and wedding before my father realised what was happening."

"Really?"

"Let me tell you, she is usually two steps ahead of everyone when it comes to manipulating any event or happening in her favour."

Suzanna was silent for a moment.

Then she remarked. "I wish I were like her."

I smiled at the thought. . .Suzanna was exactly like her.

Shortly after our arrival in Tignes, Suzanna and several other skiers departed for a competition in Bermio. While she was away, I moved out the hotel and into the British team's residence. I also acquired a large, double room so

Suzanna could share it with me. . .if she wanted to.

Again, I had that feeling of solitude. I missed her, yet, at the same time, the irrational concern welled up inside that our relationship was based on the flimsiest of foundations, and could likely fizzle out.

I phoned her late at night on several occasions. On one I got no reply.

Damn it. . .she should be in her room. Why isn`t she in her room? The thought she might be in someone else`s room ran through my mind. Eventually, common sense prevailed.

However, I did call her the next morning, at six o`clock.

A tired voice said, "Hello?"

"Hello darling, it`s me. Did I wake you?"

"Adam, you know you woke me. Is everything OK? Has something happened?" Concern was in her voice.

"Er, no, everything is fine." I suddenly remembered the Women`s Super G was taking place later in the day. "I phoned to wish you good luck."

"Oh, darling, thank you. You had me worried for a moment. We celebrated Lisa`s third place in the slalom last night. Hopefully, we`ll do the same again tonight, if I can get on the podium."

So that`s why she wasn`t in her room.

"Phone me, let me know how you get on as soon as possible." I hesitated. "I love you," I said quietly.

"What was that? I missed what you said then."

"Nothing special. I`ll speak to you later. Goodbye darling."

Did I really say that. It just came out. As if I had no control over my thoughts and feelings.

I had just returned from the slopes. In fact, I could have put more effort into it. Although parts of my body ached, I had that buoyant feeling knowing I could have pushed myself even more. After a hot bath, and an uncomfortable cold shower, I was lying on the bed when the phone rang.

"I made it! I made it! What about that?"

"Brilliant! What a clever girl! Now enjoy the celebrations. I'll be thinking of you, my love."

There it was again. What was I saying? Although, in her excitement she probably missed my emphasis on those last few words.

Over the next few days I made four practice runs on the downhill course. The discomfort of stressing my body had almost gone, and the exhilaration of pain-free skiing also improved confidence that I could give good account of myself in the GB Championships Downhill.

Moreover, I had started running again.

In doing so I became more aware that Tignes was not the prettiest resort in the Alps. The concept of a sweet alpine village was non-existent. The town looked like a part of Benidorm stuck on the side of a mountain. Unattractive blocks, built in the 1960s, made up much of the accommodation.

The town planners were trying hard to rectify past sins, and Tignes has undergone a multi-million-pound facelift in recent years. Roads that used to run through the resort have been buried in underground tunnels, and a number of new buildings and chalets has been built to accommodate visitors' needs. Running through the town I noted that some hotels were even sticking wooden cladding on their exteriors in an attempt to make them prettier.

I jogged the last hundred metres and was walking through the reception area, when my spirits were suddenly dampened by the sight of Josh Finden rising languidly from a chair and striding towards me. In an instant all the bitter memories of the incident in Aspen flooded back. I had expected Josh to come to Tignes, yet was disconcerted to see him.

"Adam, my boy, how are you? I see you`re getting back to fitness. Just in time for your home championships." He pumped my hand, while murmuring. "Is there somewhere we can talk?"

"Better come up to my room. That`s as private as anywhere."

Neither of us uttered a word as we took the lift and walked along the corridor.

"This is it. . .room two–three–nine."

I inserted the key card and pushed open the door, ushering Josh in before me.

He looked round the room. "No mini-bar, I suppose?"

"Fraid not."

Dropping into a chair he crossed his legs.

I sat opposite on another chair, unconsciously leaning forward to hear what he had to say. But before he began, I asked in a low voice. "What did you do with the body, Josh?"

"Oh, that. It was taken care of, no worries."

"What do you mean, no worries? Of course, I`m worried. When you`re caught up in an exchange of gunfire and someone gets killed, the authorities must be involved!"

"Keep your voice down, Adam." He uncrossed his legs and tweaked the crease of his trousers. "I repeat, it was satisfactorily dealt with. The guy was a known mugger, and on several occasions it seems he has totted a firearm, as he did on the night in question. I reported what happened to an attorney I know, that you and Suzanna were on the point of being shot, until I stepped in."

"And another thing. . .What on earth were you doing at that time of night with a pistol? I'm grateful. . .of course I'm grateful, but I just don't understand how you came to be there."

"Put it down as protecting my assets. You've got a great future as a downhiller, my boy, and I want to pave the way for you. If there is a mugger about to do you harm, I would be foolish to allow it. I should add as both Greg Nichols and Lars Oestensson were at the crud party, I was there to ensure my skiers got back safely to their hotel."

He smiled. "But I didn't come here to talk about Aspen, forget what happened. It's water under the bridge. I just wanted to tell you that Greg will be participating in your championships. That's all."

He rose to his feet. "Now, I'm heading to the nearest bar, will you join me?"

"Thank you, no. I'm hot and sweaty after the run, and need a shower and a rest before dinner."

"OK, my boy, I'll catch up with you later."

The door closed silently behind him.

I don't know who had the tightest grip.

We both held on to each other as soon as the coach came to a halt, and Suzanna came down the steps.

"Fantastic. . . bloody fantastic!" I said into her mass of

blond hair.

Eventually, we broke loose, much to the amusement of the rest of the team.

Todd Stewart came over. "I must say our number one Super Girl did a remarkable performance in Bermio. In fact, everyone acquitted themselves extremely well. As performance director I was really proud."

Suzanna leaned forward and kissed him on the cheek. "Thanks to your advice and encouragement, Todd."

I collected her bags and took her up to my room.

"So you`ve decided to slum it with the rest of us have you?" she grinned.

Suzanna threw herself on the bed, and put out her arms beckoning me to join her. I held her hand while we lay side by side.

I was not aware of the sigh of contentment having Suzanna beside me.

"What was that, a suppressed groan of pain?" she said, propping herself on an elbow and studying my face.

"If you must know it was the soft murmuring of a joyful man. I`m pleased you`re back, I missed you."

"Did you really?" Suzanna was staring at me intently.

"Mm. . . there`s only one fly in the ointment, Josh Finden is here."

She sat up straight.

"Have you spoken to him?"

I nodded.

"What did he have to say about Aspen?"

"When I tackled him about the incident, he was quite blasé. He said from his days as a professional skier he knew how these crud parties might get out of hand. As a consequence, he was patrolling the area around the Jermyn Hotel ready to protect those in the Finden stable.

When he saw us about to be gunned down, he took extreme action."

"Did he report it to the authorities?"

"Josh didn`t, but he said the body was transferred to a private mortuary, and all the gruesome details were given to an attorney, who, in turn, submitted a report to the police. He went on to say that he left Aspen the following day to fly to Europe. The attorney contacted him later to say the police were not taking any action, for it was the body of a well-known criminal, known to mug people at gunpoint. So, I guess that clears up the matter."

Suzanna just raised her eyebrows.

CHAPTER TWENTY-FIVE

I felt the strength coming back in my legs and upper body. Each day I had taken to the slopes putting in yet more practice on what would be, the downhill course. By degrees my confidence was returning; I now believed I could put up a reasonable show in our home championships.

Being a strong skier, it was a joy to be with Suzanna on the slopes. Moreover, having done well in Bermio, she was equally confident, and looked forward to the Women`s Super G.

Over the weekend we had dinner with Josh Finden, Greg Nichols, Lars Oestensson and several of his other clients participating in the GB Championships. Although, nominally, a British tournament, it also attracted a sprinkling of international skiers, which made it more of an event.

Josh was in an avuncular mood, advising his protégés on what to expect when skiing in Tignes, and entertaining us all with stories and anecdotes of when he was a professional skier. Towards the end of a very convivial evening, Josh took me aside and said, "Some time during the week, perhaps we could have a chat on how things are going, for my secretary reminded me that the contract you and I have is coming up for renewal shortly. What do you say to Tuesday afternoon, after Suzanna has competed in the Super G?"

"Fine by me, Josh," I replied. Though I was feeling I ought to speak with Suzanna before I signed with him.

Over the weekend we skied the hill on which the Super G would be held. Although the actual course would not be made known to the competitors until just before the race on Tuesday.

We were in the bedroom Sunday evening when Suzanna began removing her clothes from the wardrobe, collecting up cosmetics and other items and stuffing everything in her suitcase.

"What are you doing? Are you leaving? What`s going on?" I asked, now fearing that the unwarranted dread she might feel it had all been a ghastly mistake, was suddenly a reality.

She came round to my side of the bed.

"Adam I`m just taking things back to my room. I had a message today that my parents are coming to Tignes to see me race on Tuesday. At some point, they may well come to my room, and it would look odd if were bare. I`ll just scatter things around, and be back."

She stood looking down at me, as I sat frozen in a chair.

Her face took on a serious look. "You thought I was leaving you, didn`t you?"

I nodded, not properly able to articulate my thoughts.

Her eyes moistened.

"Idiot. . .I`ve invested too much of my emotional soul

in you to walk away now," she murmured, taking my face in her hands, "Listen carefully, though I shall probably say it many times over, you are the one for me — understood? I`ll admit there have been moments when I`ve wondered if things were happening too quickly. That the passion of the moment might simply evaporate. But it hasn`t. . .it has got stronger. So, now you know," she sniffed.

I stood up and wrapped my arms around her.

Swaying together gently, I whispered in her ear. "I love you, Miss Bancroft."

She burst into tears.

I saw little of Suzanna on Monday.

She spent much of the day with her parents, and I met them, Veronica and Richard, for dinner in the evening.

They were a delightful couple. Her mother was vivacious, amusing, and appeared young for her age. An insight to how Suzanna would be twenty-five years on. Her father was quieter, more measured in his manner and speech. At times I had the feeling I was being assessed, not in an unkind way, but subtly checking I was right for his daughter. I would have done the same in his position.

We walked them back to the Hotel Village Montana, where they had booked in for the week.

I mentioned that whilst Tignes had its attractions, they may well find Val d`Isère, further down the Tarentaise Valley, more inviting. Though both are essentially dormitory towns, catering principally for visitors during both the winter and summer seasons. Suzanna mentioned we had a car, and she could drive them there if they fancied the idea. They welcomed the offer, and it was agreed they would go on Wednesday, after women's Super G the previous day.

I would not be joining them, as I was competing in the preliminary rounds of the downhill, leading up to the final on Saturday.

I stood with her parents at the barrier encircling the runout.

I believe I was more nervous than Suzanna. She had prepared well, and really there was no need to feel anxious. She was skiing in fifteenth place, so the snow condition would be acceptable, not too many ruts or bumps to throw her off line. Still, I could not control my anxiety, moving from one foot to the other, staring fixedly at the distant starting gate through binoculars, waiting for the moment she would burst through the wand and hurtle down towards the finish.

I could see her clearly when she was in the starting hut and took her place at the gate: the marshal counting down the last few seconds.

Suddenly she pitched forward, the wand brushed aside, poles thrust into the snow for extra leverage, as Suzanna catapulted herself down the slope.

I was clapping my hands, and yelling encouragement, until I realised both Suzanna's parents were staring at me wide-eyed. I grinned sheepishly; but moments later I felt compelled to shout her name and kick the barrier.

She sailed through the gates, skiing with style and assurance.

My heart was in my mouth. She must have posted an outstanding time as she swept across the finish line...and she had! One minute, four point eight six seconds. The same time as Lindsey Voss posted when she won the Super G.

She came to a halt, leant over the barrier and hugged Angela and Richard.

Then she turned to me.

I could hardly say anything, I was too full.

Suzanna removed her helmet, and kissed me. . .long and hard.

Finally, I found my voice. "Brilliant. . .absolutely brilliant!"

And so it proved. She won by nine tenths of a second, a country mile in this sort of competition.

The following day I joined other skiers training for the Downhill.

We boarded the cable car that would take us up to the lofty Grande Motte glacier. Although everyone's thoughts were concentrated on what lay ahead, at three thousand five hundred metres, we were provided with a 360-degree view of one of the most beautiful panoramas in the French Alps.

Now the slopes had been prepared for the event, and were banned to all except the downhill competitors. On the initial run my aim was to ski the course faster than previous outings, but to save a fair bit in reserve. Come Thursday, I wanted to be in the top ten, and more assured of an early run, free from too many bumps and ridges.

As a consequence, I was taking few chances, and skied an acceptable time, though not nearly as quick as some of the others. Now the course was event ready, it was a pleasurable descent and took no great effort on my part.

Suzanne and her parents were standing close to the barrier at the runout.

"Why were you dawdling? I thought you wanted a fast time." she queried.

I removed my helmet, and grinned at her.

"I do, but now the course is in top condition, without ruts or divots, I wanted to be exact on the line I'm taking, not rush headlong down to the finish."

Her father remarked. "Well, it looked jolly fast to me."

"You wait 'til Saturday, Dad," she said, "that's when you'll see what I mean. Adam was quite slow on this run."

Thursday dawned.

When I looked out the bedroom window, it was a clear, bright sky, no wind, ideal for producing a fast time. I turned towards the bed to tell Suzanna what the weather was like. She was not there. Even though her parents were staying elsewhere, Suzanna said they might phone or need to contact her. She would not want them to know we slept together. . .not yet anyway. As a consequence, she occupied her own room.

At night I would accompany Suzanna up to the first floor, kiss her chastely goodnight at the bedroom door, and retire to mine on the floor above. I was not even allowed in her room. Somehow, her attitude appealed to me. She had had a separate room when at my parents' home; and although out of step with the current times, her view was that it saved embarrassment for all concerned.

She was already at the breakfast table when I entered the dining room. I took a chair and smiled at her. "A great day for skiing," I remarked.

"What time does the downhill session start?" Suzanna asked.

"Twelve thirty, I`ve plenty of time to make sure my skis have not been tampered with," I replied, stealing a piece of her toast.

"Mm. . .do you want me to check them as well?"

"No, a kind offer, but that won`t be necessary. I`ll go over them thoroughly, and then not let them out of my sight. Are you taking your parents anywhere today?"

"Perhaps this afternoon, after your training run," Suzanna said, slapping my hand as I stretched it out to spirit away another slice of toast. "Why don`t you join us?"

"Where were you thinking of going?"

"Some years ago Father visited Les Brevières, it`s just outside Tignes, past Lac du Chevril. He particularly remembers the crêpes he enjoyed there, and fancied another visit."

"I like crêpes, I`ll come with you."

I took my place in the starting hut and shuffled forward towards the gate as skiers departed at two-minute intervals. Then it was my turn. The starter counted off the last few seconds, I broke through the wand, accelerated hard, and raced down the slope adopting a racing position.

Twisting, turning, working my edges, I maintained the planned line of descent. Now I could see the red archway housing the finishing line just twenty seconds away. Yet more speed, forget the tormented legs. I lunged for the line and swept into the runout, coming to a hockey stop opposite Suzanna and her parents.

As I removed my helmet, she called. "Well done! You're in third position, Adam!"

And I stayed there, even when all the others had completed their runs. So I would be in the first ten in the downhill on Saturday.

As we were leaving the course, Josh Finden appeared. "A first-class run, Adam. You'll be difficult to beat on Saturday."

"How did your other skiers fare, Josh?" I had already scanned the top thirty list, and knew only Greg Nichols was in with a chance.

He shrugged and raised his eyebrows. "They'll come good . . . early days yet."

With that he moved away to talk to someone.

We drove to Les Brevières, visited the crêperie, which Richard thoroughly enjoyed; and returned to Tignes in time for the draw to determine in what position I would skiing on Saturday.

After an evening meal Suzanna's parents left us, and we went on to the Melting Pot, a night club on Rue du Val Claret. As now accustomed, several hours later, I saw Suzanna dutifully to her room, then walked up the stairs to mine.

Opening the door, I had not realised the lights and the television had been left on. But then a figure rose from one of the comfortable chairs, and murmured. "Hello, Adam, you're later than I expected."

It was Alexei Sokolov.

"What the hell are you doing here?"

He merely smiled and replied, "I was in Geneva, and thought I`d call upon you."

"Really? That`s over two hundred kilometres away."

"I wanted to talk to you, Adam. Not by phone, such conversations have ears. Moreover, I knew you would not miss skiing in the British Championships. It was a simple matter to track you down."

Recovering from the shock of his appearance, my senses were now alert to any sudden act. I said. "Would you like a drink? I think I could do with one."

"You don`t have a minibar, I`ve checked," Alexei said.

"No, we could go down to the bar, or I can phone for room service."

"Let`s just have a quiet drink in the room."

I phoned, and shortly afterwards two large whiskies arrived.

"Your continued health, my friend," Alexei tipped his glass in my direction.

There was a companionable silence until I eventually said. "So, driving all the way from Geneva suggests you have something important to tell me."

"You`re right, of course. In fact several items of information."

Sokolov drank from his glass. "Do you remember when we had the idea the Russian Mafia were somehow involved with UPS? Well the company`s main distribution centre and offices are located in Derbenevskaya Business Park in Moscow. It was the simplest matter to keep the place under surveillance, and we did so for over a fortnight. The result, we now know, was a dead end."

"So, if it's not the parcel carrier it must be the `Unterstützungsfond Für Professional Skiläufer`.

"Yes, `The Professional Skiers` Benevolent Fund`. Tell me, in your opinion, is it a front for something criminal?"

"Hard to say. It appears to do good works, particularly for those after their skiing days are over, and have fallen on hard times."

"Mm. . . but it could be, and that's why Vasiliev mentioned UPS in his dying breath?" murmured Sokolov.

"He also mouthed microswitch," I added.

"Yes, you mentioned that earlier. I've had a few thoughts on that one. Tell me, are you competing in World Cup Championships in Val d'Isère?"

"Hopefully, now the event has been put back to the end of the season rather than at the beginning because of a lack of snow. I have to convince the British Team performance director that I'm fit enough. . .and that's what I intend to do in our home event."

"Good, I've got a room at Les Barmes de L'Ours during the championships. We must get together. However, beforehand, I have to go to Lucerne. It has been suggested that a certain Leonid Davidenko has financial dealings there. I want to dig up whatever I can about him."

"Who is he?" I asked.

"Davidenko, Adam, is the head of Bratva."

"Bratva. . .what is that, another of your recently privatised companies?"

Sokolov smiled grimly. "Bratva, my good friend, is the Russian Mafia, and Davidenko is their top man!"

CHAPTER TWENTY-SIX

Saturday dawned under another clear blue sky.

I went down a floor and knocked on Suzanna`s door.

Jeff Rivers, our slalom specialist, passed me in the corridor. He grinned when I knocked again.

"Suzanna`s downstairs, Adam, chatting to Lars Oestensson."

"Right, thank you, Jeff."

What was Oestensson doing in Tignes? Had he come to see Suzanna?

As I made my way to the dining room, jealousy and irritation in equal measure welled up and drowned any thoughts I had about the downhill. Never before had I had these feelings, until I met Suzanna.

I threaded my way through the tables and stood for a moment behind Oestensson, while Suzanna was laughing at something he had said. Looking up she saw the cast of my face. Her eyes flickered before she, too, got to her feet.

"Darling, there you are. Lars was just telling me of an incident in his last race."

"I see. I won`t stop, I`ve already eaten. I think I`ll start getting my things together, check my skis and equipment.

I'll catch up with you later."

With that I turned on my heel and left the dining room.

I was fuming. Bloody Lars Oestensson was chatting up my girl. As Josh Finden had remarked on a previous occasion, he was a fast worker. What the hell was he doing here?

I strode out the main door and started walking towards the lake. My mind so occupied with the situation, it took some minutes to realise I was not dressed for the outside. I was shivering uncontrollably. Moreover, having missed breakfast, I was now extremely hungry. Not the best way to get ready for the race.

I was still preoccupied by Oestensson's intrusion and the fact that Suzanna seemed to delight in his company when I took the cable car to the summit of the Grande Motte glacier. The Downhill was recently renamed the Johan Clarey run, for the locally-born French skier was the first person to break the 100mph barrier during a World Cup race. The skier clocked 100.6mph during the Wengen Downhill in Switzerland. I would not be anywhere near that speed today, though I was so incensed by this morning's episode, I was ready to try.

Throughout the preliminaries, my mind was buzzing. I was barely aware of the other skiers. Eventually, I shuffled into the starting hut, behind those swaying to their recall of the course.

Then it was my turn.

Poised at the gate.

The official counted down the seconds with his fingers.

When the last digit came down, I lurched forward

breaking through the wand, I rammed my poles into the snow, straining every muscle to gain acceleration.

I don`t remember much of the run. Having skied the course so often I was on autopilot. My attention more on why I was put out by Oestensson`s appearance and Suzanna`s obvious delight in his presence.

All the time Angela and I were together, I was never troubled when others paid her close attention. We had lived together for several years, during which there were frequent occasions when I would spend time in the company of other women. But it went no further; nor would the advances made upon Angela have led to anything.

Suddenly, I was aware of the looming finish line.

In that moment I also recognised two things. Suzanna had committed herself to me: she was not seeking other admirers. I was playing the injured party like a naïve teenager.

"Grow up, Livesey!" I shouted coming to a halt in the runout.

Off came the helmet, as I searched for Suzanna.

"Suzanna!" I shouted.

Then she appeared at the barrier. Removing my skis I ran to her.

"Darling, I`m sorry I was boorish this morning."

She heard me, but her attention was fixed on the race board.

"Look up there!"

I turned my head and saw I was in the lead by close to one and a half seconds.

"Wow, Adam, you`ve never skied as fast as that before!" she cried.

Reluctantly, I took the leading skier`s position on the

dais. But I would rather have been by her side.

When the last competitor had skied the course I was still in the lead by three-quarters of a second.

More importantly, Suzanna had dismissed my earlier behaviour; that was what really mattered.

Josh came over and congratulated me, as did a number of other skiers, including Oestensson. Truth to tell, I did not like the man; but logic prevailed, and I shook his hand.

We joined Todd Stewart and members of the British team for dinner in the evening, and Suzanna and I sat either side of the performance director. We were talking about technique, when Todd remarked. "Have you ever thought of using a wind tunnel, Adam?"

"Interesting you should say that, Todd. I was reading about cyclists using wind tunnels to hone their riding positions," said Suzanna. "Apparently, even minor adjustments can minimise wind resistance. In fact, there is such a set-up at Southampton University, we ought to try it, Adam."

A chance remark, which blossomed into staying with Suzanna's parents, and skiing into an artificial wind.

CHAPTER TWENTY-SEVEN

We had both promised Todd that we would be back in Tignes before Suzanna left to participate in a women's Super G competition at Sestriere, in Northern Italy. As she was the only one of the British team competing, I was going to accompany her.

Arriving at London Heathrow Airport, I hired a car and drove the forty-five-minute journey to Oxford. I had phoned earlier and asked if Suzanna and I could stay the night. My mother welcomed us, my father nodded in our direction and carried on reading either an autobiography or the memoirs of a politician, both his favourite reading.

"One room or two?" Mother enquired over her shoulder as we followed her up the stairs.

I glimpsed Suzanna blush, but she took the initiative. "One, please Mrs Livesey, it will create less work."

Mother nodded. "Well, you'd better take one of what used to be the girls' rooms, they're more spacious and the beds are larger."

Then she asked. "Tell me, why exactly have you come to Oxford. You mumbled something on the phone, Adam, but I didn't catch it."

"I want to collect my spare skiing gear. Suzanna and I

are going to subject ourselves to a wind tunnel at Southampton University, to see if we can improve the aerodynamics of our skiing. We've been told it will help to streamline our posture. If you don't mind Mother, we'll be on our way immediately after breakfast."

Suzanna's parents lived in Hampshire in the village of Kings Somborne. Suzanna directed me to a large Georgian house standing well back from the road in spacious grounds.

"What a splendid building," I remarked, captivated by the well-tended lawns, shrubberies and an abundance of trees which seemed to enclose the property.

"I love to be near trees," I said wistfully, thinking back to my youth when, on a Summer's evening, I would clamber through an opening in the fence into University Parks. The gates would be shut, no one was about, and I would sit for an hour or so beneath my favourite oak.

"So do I," grinned Suzanna, "but there is a certain time of year that casts father into deep despair. From the middle of October to mid-December he is like a bear with a sore head. All because he has to clear up the leaves; and believe me, there are great mounds of them. He says they refuse to burn and take years to compost. So he and the gardener have to clear them up, fill plastic bags and wheelbarrow them down to the entrance gates, where a contractor takes them away. I don't think we shall visit home between October and December."

Interesting. . .so she is thinking that far ahead.

I parked the car outside the building housing the wind tunnels.

We had been fortunate that Suzanna`s father, Richard, had several friends on the engineering faculty at the university, which had paved our way for an early appointment with the technical people operating the site.

Welcomed by the team, we were first shown around the building which offered three different types of tunnel. The largest, called the R J Mitchell tunnel, after the creator of the famous Spitfire fighter plane, would be ideal for our purpose.

Suzanna and I were told that research carried out using the wind tunnel had assisted the British cycling team as well as others involved in performance related sports. We explained what we had in mind, and while getting into our skiing gear technicians fixed my skis to the floor.

"I think I ought to go in first," I said to Suzanna, "just in case there`s a slight mishap."

"If you wish," she responded, "though I can`t see any likelihood of being blown off my feet."

I was accompanied into the tunnel by another technician called Robert.

Clicking home the bindings, and standing up, I experienced the oddest sensation. Normally, when donning skis there is subtle movement when on snow and ice. You automatically adjust your stance; but in the tunnel your feet are completely rigid.

"A couple of things I need to check," said Robert. "Your speed range and the likely field temperature. We can run the fan to reflect speeds of four to forty metres a second. Tops, over ninety miles an hour. What do you reach coming off the slopes?"

"Usually, we come out the starting gate and hit about

eighty to ninety miles an hour in the first fifty metres. It depends on where we are, what mountain we are riding. We often slow to fifty miles an hour on some of the tight turns."

"So we'll start from zero and push it quickly up to forty metres a second. What about the temperature on the mountains?"

"Anything from one degree Celsius to five, so the body temperature is low, though it quickly rises to about thirty-eight degrees due to the exertion."

"Mm, so it's cool air for the most part?"

"Yes."

"Right, to begin with, we'll just run it at a gentle speed, say ten metres a second while you get the feel of the tunnel. When you wave an arm we shall shut it down. Wave again when you're ready to raise it quickly to forty metres. OK?"

I nodded, and went to put on my helmet.

"Before you don the headgear," said Robert, "we shall be recording your body positions with a Nutem scanning and PIV system for optical measurements of the airflow. We'll run the tunnel at top speed for twenty seconds, then back to thirty metres per second for the next fifteen seconds. Finally for ten seconds at twenty metres a second. Then we'll analyse your profile at the different speeds on the recording. We shall consider if any adjustments need to be made to your posture and if there are, you can adopt them on the second run in the tunnel, to discover if there are any improvements aerodynamically."

"Thanks, Robert."

He nodded again, and went out through the unobtrusive door in the tunnel wall.

Suddenly the giant fan began to rotate, gradually

increasing speed. As it rose, I automatically leant into the wind and adopted my usual skiing stance. It was cool air blowing, slowly becoming colder.

Ten metres a second would be equivalent to idling on the slopes. I experienced the stiff breeze for a few minutes before raising my arm. The fan came unhurriedly to a halt.

Now I adopted my usual crouch as though at the starting gate. I felt for my poles, a reflex action. I was not going anywhere. . .anywhere was coming to me.

The fan started spinning, building up rapidly. Even wearing a helmet the sound was loud. I bent further against the strengthening wind. I wondered, briefly, if the bindings would work if I were pitched backwards.

The twenty seconds seemed an age, but there was a slight let-up in the wind velocity and I adopted the usual lean when racing down a thirty degree slope.

Shortly afterwards the fan slowed perceptibly and I was coasting as though into the runout.

All was quiet.

The side door opened and Robert appeared.

"OK?" he asked.

It took a moment to get my breath back. I had not realised how demanding the exertion of skiing into the wind would be. I undid the bindings and walked slowly towards the exit.

There were several technicians in the control room who had a clear view of events in the tunnel. Peering through the window I could see Suzanna`s skis being fixed to the floor.

Suzanna stood beside me. "What`s it like?" she asked quietly.

"Fairly straightforward, but it`s a strange feeling at

first with skis you don't slide. Robert will ask you questions about skiing a Super G, such things as speed and temperature, and your answers will largely dictate how fast the fan turns. But it's certainly not daunting."

Robert joined us. "Ready when you are, Miss Bancroft. Shall we go in?"

I watched as she was installed in the tunnel. I could see their lips moving, but could not hear what was said.

Suzanna adopted the same routine as me, only the speeds were slower. Ten minutes later she came through the tunnel door and Robert ushered both of us to another part of the control room.

"I'll now show you your profiles which are defined by the air flow coursing around your bodies. Let's take yours first, Adam," he said, turning to the large screen monitor.

Suddenly, I appeared on the screen. I moved into a casual tuck position when the fan was running at ten metres a second. At this stage I could see the air flow over me was broken and irregular.

"Now we come to what might be regarded as exiting the starting gate," he explained.

This was the rapid increase in speed to forty metres a second.

I tucked my body lower, kept my elbows tight to my body, and moved my arms forward. The flow was infinitely better, though my arms, without the poles in my hands, looked a little low.

"Now I'll show you the overhead view," Robert declared.

On the screen appeared the air streaming either side of my body. It was immediately obvious that the right arm was not so neatly tucked in as the left. As a consequence, there was an interrupted flow around the elbow clear for all to see.

I made the comment. "It might be because I did not have the poles with me."

"Did you bring them with you?"

"Yes, they're in the car."

"Well, on the next run tuck them under your arms," said Robert. "Then we can judge if your right elbow is usually a little more adrift. If it is, over the course you might be adding a couple of tenths of a second. . .could be significant. The other thing I noticed in the tuck position is your hands. I believe they should be higher, almost in line with your nose."

It was Suzanna's turn.

We could not see any fault in her tuck; elbows nice and tight; she looked well-balanced on her skis. Perhaps the only comment might be that she was a fraction slow to go into a tuck position at the start.

I retrieved the poles from the car and had a second session in the tunnel.

To my surprise, even with the poles the elbow was still marginally turned outwards. In future I must make a conscious effort to keep it closer to my upper body. I even had to raise my hands a fraction to be in line with my nose.

When the fan stopped, I asked if they could create a profile of when I encounter the jumps. This demands a different posture, where you drop your arms, so they hang either side of your body.

The results. . .for me, my hands should be higher, and an adjustment to the right arm: let it not wander when it should be tight to my body. There was no need to adjust any part of me when in a jumping position.

Everything was OK with Suzanna, though they

suggested she should get into the tuck position more quickly at the starting gate. A worthwhile trip, and I had much to thank Todd Stewart for recommending it.

Returning to Suzanna`s parents` home we explained the benefits of using a wind tunnel to make, albeit minor improvements; but in a sport where hundredths of a second count, the time spent in the wind tunnel had been invaluable.

CHAPTER TWENTY-EIGHT

I drove into the underground car park and left the car in my allotted bay. Carrying my spare ski equipment, Suzanna and I took the lift to the third floor, and walked along the corridor to my flat.

"This is a pleasant part of London, Adam," she remarked as I dumped everything on the carpeted floor to search for my keys. "How long have you lived here?"

Inserting the right one in the lock, I replied. "I`ve had the flat for about three years, but, as you know, much of the time I`m travelling around Europe. I don`t get to use it as often as I would like."

As I gathered up my things Suzanna preceded me, and strolled into the living room. "What a lovely room, and such a good size. How big is it?"

"It`s got all the usual facilities, bathroom, kitchen, and two bedrooms. Have a wander round."

Ten minutes later she came back into the sitting room. "It`s great. Who did the decoration?"

"Well, I did most of it, though one of my sisters gave me a hand."

"Mm, I like your taste. This is exactly the sort of décor I would have chosen."

I walked over to her and took her in my arms. "Good, because I hope you'll see it often in the future. Particularly, in the bedroom."

Suzanna laughed and kissed me. "I shall look forward to admiring its ceiling, from a strategic position."

"You are incorrigible, Miss Bancroft," I whispered in her ear.

"Hopefully, Mr Livesey."

We stayed locked together, swaying gently for a while, until I said the welcome word. "Tea, darling?"

"I thought you'd never ask."

I made tea and added biscuits to the tray. When I returned, Suzanna was viewing the books displayed on floor to ceiling shelves.

"The majority seem to be history books, Adam. Is that a subject you particularly enjoy?" she asked over her shoulder. "That and religion, I see. Are you a religious person?"

"Yes to the history, and truth to tell, I suppose I could be described as an atheist. I find all religions intellectually insupportable. Most of those debunk the notion of a Supreme Being. I think I've got all Richard Dawkins' books."

"You'd better not tell my father. He's an ardent churchgoer. It wouldn't do for his daughter to be keen on an unbeliever," she said, laughing at the thought.

We sat together on the settee holding hands.

"Another cup?"

"Please."

I came back from the kitchen and put the mugs on the coffee table.

Then I went into the hall to collect the mail, which had accumulated during my absence.

Much of it was instantly disposable; and the rest of no great interest, except two letters, both featuring Swiss postmarks. One was immediately recognisable, a slogan on the envelope identified the sender as `Die Versicherungs Gesellschaft der Luzern` — The Insurance Company Of Lucerne. I opened it to find a cheque for the difference in the excess payment, and a brief letter of apology for a clerical oversight from the health insurance division, `Luzerner Krankenkasse`.

The other, whatever it was, was in a plain envelope. When opened, it contained a receipt for my donation to the `Unterstützungsfond Für Professional Skiläufer` — the `Benevolent Fund for Professional Skiers`.

I passed the first letter, with the attached cheque, to Suzanna. "The insurance company realised the error of their ways." I remarked. "The other one is a receipt for a donation I made recently."

I put it on the table and drank my tea.

I watched as Suzanna picked up the receipt and laid it next to the cheque. She appeared to be studying the two items. I sat back and relaxed, cradling the mug in both hands.

"Adam," she said after a few minutes, "look at this."

I eased along the settee and peered over her shoulder.

"Look closely at the two signatures. To my mind they both belong to the same person."

I studied them for a minute or so. "There is a similarity. . .but one looks like `Markovich`, and the other, that`s possibly, `Miklovich`."

"Have you got a magnifying glass?"

I stood up. "Yes. . .somewhere."

I went into the kitchen and rummaged through several drawers before I found what she wanted.

Suzanna stared intently at the two signatures. She put down the glass and quietly remarked. "They're slightly fuzzy because they are printed on the documents, but I'd bet you anything they are both signatures of K. Miklovich, whoever that is."

It was my turn to stare. "My God, I told you that before he died Anatoly Vasiliev mumbled two words, `microswitch` and `UPS`. We now believe the latter was the `Professional Skiers' Benevolent Fund`. The other, well, I could not understand what he was getting at with `microswitch`."

I unconsciously stroked my chin. "But perhaps he was trying to say, `Miklovich`. Is he Russian do you think? On reflection, I suppose he could be any nationality, even Swiss. I'll speak to Sokolov. If it's a Russian name, he might know who it is."

Twenty-four hours later we were back in Tignes, only to learn from Todd that the weather in Sestriere was so atrocious, most of the events had been cancelled.

It's odd how chance can play a major role in one's plans, and send you off in a completely different direction. I phoned Alexei Sokolov — I had his personal cell phone number.

"Adam, my friend, this is a pleasant surprise. What can I do for you?"

"I won't keep you Alexei, it's just a simple query. Would the name Miklovich. . .or Markovich. . .suggest the person is Russian?"

"Why do you ask?"

"I have received a cheque and a receipt for a payment, and I`m trying to decipher the names of the signatories. . .they look remarkably similar."

"Tell me, is this a private cheque or business cheque?"

Sokolov`s voice had sharpened. Suddenly, he wanted to know details.

"Well, the cheque is issued by the `Die Versicherungs Gesellschaft der Luzern`, The Insurance Company of Lucerne, on behalf of the health insurance division, `Luzerner Krankenkasse`. It`s for an over-charge in the excess payment when I was in hospital in St. Moritz. The receipt is for my donation to the `Unterstützungsfond Für Professional Skiläufer`."

"Of course, `UPS`. Tell me, where are you at the moment?"

"Suzanna and I have just returned to Tignes from England. We were going off to Sestriere, Suzanna was competing there, but the weather has cancelled out any thoughts of that. In fact, judging by the forecast, it looks likely we shall catch unpleasant weather here shortly."

"Look, Adam, drop everything and come and see me. I`m in Lucerne at the moment, and about to head off for Sörenberg-Rothorn/Dorf, where the powder snow is excellent. What is more, it`s only fifteen kilometres from Lucerne. A taxi ride. You could use the slopes there and we could also discuss your little problem. I`m staying at the Radisson Blu hotel at the moment, I could book a room here for you and Suzanna as my guests. What do you say?"

"Just a minute, Alexei, let me have a word with Suzanna."

No more than five seconds later.

"Fine, thanks Alexei, we`ll see you at the Radisson

tomorrow lunchtime."

We left Tignes at eight o'clock the following morning, after once more assuring Todd we would be back well before the FIS World Cup Championships in Val d'Isère. It was a long drive to Lucerne, passing through Geneva and Bern. After desultory conversation for an hour or so, Suzanna was suddenly silent. I glanced across to find she had fallen asleep. One minute she was talking, the next she was dead to the world. I had noticed whenever a passenger on a plane, train or in a car, she invariably falls asleep. It is when, whatever form of transport comes to a standstill, she promptly awakens and asks where are we.

Predictably, when I pulled into the hotel's underground car park and turned off the engine, she came alive.

"Where are we?" she murmured.

"Guess."

She gazed out the window. "Haven't a clue," she replied.

"We are at the Radisson Blu in Lucerne."

"How can that be? I only dozed off for a short while."

"That little while was almost four hours, Miss Bancroft."

We made our way through the dining room to a far corner where Alexei was sitting. As we neared the table he rose, shook my hand, and kissed Suzanna's cheek.

"Good to see you, my friends, we have much to discuss. But first we must order."

With that he lifted a hand and an attentive waiter

drifted over.

Neither Suzanna nor I were that hungry. We both requested omelettes. I was surprised to see Alexei choosing several courses, and another bottle of wine in addition to one already on the table.

Once the waiter had departed, Alexei plied us with, from what I could see of the label, a very decent red. Then he raised his glass towards us in salute. "To you both. . .thanks for making the journey to Lucerne."

"You mentioned powder snow on the slopes," I grinned across the table, "what greater incentive would we need? Seriously though, what was so pressing, Alexei?"

He leaned across the table and stared at me for a brief moment.

"What you said on the phone may well shed a great deal of light on Vasiliev`s death. . .or should I call it murder."

His voice dropped to a whisper.

"You`ll recall I set up a surveillance team to monitor the `UPS` headquarters in the business park south of Moscow. The aim was to note the comings and goings of people working there. There are only a handful of organisations that could have taken over the company, the most likely being Bratva. . .the Russian Mafia. But also, as you know, that came to nothing."

Alexei paused to drink from his glass. He glanced in my direction, and gave a wry smile.

"Subsequently, you were of the opinion that the initials `UPS` stood for the `Professional Skiers` Benevolent Fund`."

He paused when the newly ordered second bottle arrived. The silence continued while Alexei tasted the wine and gave the sommelier a brief nod, who then poured it into our glasses before departing.

Sokolov's knowing smile switched between Suzanna and me.

"I think I have discovered what Vasiliev meant when he uttered, the words, 'microswitch'. In fact, your two letters could very well confirm it. If you have them with you, could I see them, Adam?"

I passed the envelopes to Alexei, who carefully removed their contents, and spread them out on the table in front of him. Like Suzanna, he drew a magnifying glass from a pocket to enlarge the images.

While he was engrossed in studying the documents, our meals were served. Suzanna and I just sat there while Alexei continued to study the documents. He was so absorbed they remained untouched.

Eventually, he looked up and in a calm voice said. "There is little doubt, these two signatures are the hand of the same person. You mentioned that UPS might well be operating in the same building as The Lucerne Insurance Company. . .you could well be right."

"The initials on an office door were only a poorly, hand-written notice," Suzanna commented. "It was quite small, probably to alert the insurance company staff that another business was operating in their midst."

"Well, digging deeper, I traced the skiers' fund to Morgartenstrasse, which is close to the railway station and Lucerne's Culture and Convention Centre. However, when I went there, I found it was an accommodation address. A questionable law firm providing registered office facilities, nothing more. So. . .your 'UPS' could be operating cheek by jowl with `Die Versicherungs Gesellschaft der Luzern` . . .and Mr Boris Miklovich, that's the name on your cheque and on the receipt, would appear to be the CEO of both organisations!"

"Is that legal?" queried Suzanna.

"Highly illegal. In Switzerland the authorities are not overbearing about the setting up of charities. As a consequence, they attract a considerable number of charitable foundations. However, they are strict when there is blatant mismanagement. The law does not allow anyone with commercial interests at management level to be a director or trustee of a charitable foundation. Nor do they sanction anyone in charge of a charitable business who has a criminal record."

"Has Mr Miklovich got a criminal record?" queried Suzanna.

"Only for one or two minor offences," Alexei replied. "But they should have checked his background."

"Why is that?" I asked.

"Because, Adam, Mr Boris Miklovich is a senior member of the Bratva. . .he is the Russian Mafia's top financial man! What is more, I have been delving into the directorships of the insurance company Would you believe, it has seven board members, and five are nominees."

"What does that mean, Alexei?" questioned Suzanna.

"It means that five directors don't want to be recognised. They have appointed others to represent them, and, no doubt, carry out their wishes."

"Do we know who they really are?" I asked.

"Not at the moment," said Alexei. "But I've a good idea who one of them might be, besides Miklovich."

"How's that, if they are nominee directors?" I asked.

He grinned at me. "Did you notice the chairman is L. D. Drugoy. If it`s whom I think it is, he can`t bear to have his identity completely hidden, he`s too fond of his own importance."

Suzanna remarked. "I don`t get it. In Russian it`s, L. D. Another."

"Exactly. Is it not an English way to use the term, A N Other, when a replacement is needed? In this instance I`ll wager the `Other` is Leonid Davidenko. The *il capo* of the Russian Mafia is assuming the thinnest of disguises!"

CHAPTER TWENTY-NINE

Suzanna and I went with Alexei to Sörenberg-Rothorn/Dorf. However, we had only been there a few hours when he was called back to Lucerne.

"I`ve just received a phone call. I`m afraid I have to return to Lucerne immediately. Don`t worry, I`ll join you for dinner tonight."

With that a taxi whisked him away.

What he had said earlier was true. The skiing was invigorating without being too demanding. Both Suzanna and I enjoyed the day, and it was late afternoon when we returned to the Radisson Blu Hotel.

I was surprised to see Alexei Sokolov already at the table we had occupied at breakfast. Not only that, most of the contents of a wine bottle had been consumed.

"Welcome. . .welcome my two good friends."

I wondered, was there a slight blurring of the words?

"Come, sit, celebrate with me," Alexei drawled. "Forgive me if I seem a little light-hearted, I have much to tell you."

I glanced at Suzanna. Lightheaded might have been a more appropriate term.

"By the way," Alexei continued, "have you yet

realised that you have a bodyguard? He has been dogging your heels for a while now."

Suzanna frowned. "I thought we had agreed we did not need the services of a minder," she remarked.

"You two are important to me," Alexei murmured. "I was not going to risk losing friends who have a contract out on them. I used someone who is very discreet, I doubt you would have been aware of your protector."

"When did he start, this protector, Alexei?" I asked.

"In his role. . . after the dinner we had at the Red Fox in Rosa Khutor."

"Well, we didn't see sign of a bodyguard when we were nearly mugged in Aspen," Suzanna said crisply.

"Oh, I didn't know you were nearly mugged. What happened?" queried Alexei.

"We had just left a party; Adam and I were walking towards a distant cab rank when this guy jumped out of the shadows and drew a gun. . ."

I interrupted her. What happened was best kept to ourselves. "Fortunately, Josh Finden, my agent, was in the vicinity and scared him off."

Suzanna glanced sharply in my direction, but said nothing.

"So, where was he when needed?" I remarked.

"Mm, I'm sorry. He should have been protecting you. When I catch up with him I'll find out why," Alexei said in a low voice. Then he brightened. "Never mind, you're still here, so join me in a celebratory drink."

"What is there to celebrate?" I asked.

"Just give me a moment." He called the sommelier over and ordered champagne.

"Right, let me explain. I have already mentioned the name Miklovich, Boris Miklovich, the Bratva's money man. I was aware he comes regularly to Lucerne, and always begins his visit with a good lunch on one of the Lake Lucerne's paddle steamers. But we had no idea what he did afterwards, besides immersing himself in the affairs of The Lucerne Insurance Company, of course. I thought it worthwhile finding out what he did during the time he was here, so I decided to follow him.

"When I returned to Lucerne earlier today, it was to wait for the Stadt Luzern, the paddle steamer, to dock so I could follow Miklovich and get to know his movements. However, ten minutes before the ship came alongside the quay, a limousine drove up. To my dismay Miklovich was first off the Stadt Luzern. He walked over to the Mercedes and started talking to the driver. Presumably, telling him of his travel plans.

"One of the stewards came onto the quay to offer to passengers a hand as they disembarked. I moved towards him, more to catch what Miklovich was saying. The steward glanced in my direction, then nodded towards the car as the Bratva money man climbed into the vehicle. `One of our regulars, he comes nearly every week for a meal aboard ship,` he said.

"It was then I realised the fellow might well know a great deal more about Boris Miklovich, so I engaged him in conversation. `Obviously, he enjoys what the resident chef offers,` I remarked.

`I should say so,` the steward replied. `so much so, he's bringing all his company officials for a gourmet lunch followed by some sort of meeting in ten days' time. He has even reserved the whole ship just for the occasion, what about that?`

`You say in ten days' time, clearly, he is a wealthy man. All right for some,` I said, before walking away."

"What do you think of that?" Alexei grinned.

"What should we think?" asked Suzanna. "So he is holding a party onboard ship, what`s so significant about that?"

I studied Alexei`s face. "It means darling, his company officials are, in reality, the top brass of the Russian Mafia, and they will be congregating in Lucerne, en masse."

I glanced at Sokolov. "You`ve got something up your sleeve, haven`t you, Alexei?"

"I will have, Adam. I`ve got a plan which, if it works, will put paid to these people. . .at least for a while. Hence, the champagne, so drink to my success in putting the major players in jail for quite some time."

Suzanna and I stood up and solemnly raised our glasses in his direction.

"By the way, did you manage to catch up with Miklovich and discover his movements, Alexei?" Suzanna asked.

"Yes, I took a taxi to Haldensteig, and found the Mercedes parked by the building of The Insurance Company of Lucerne. I took a number of photos of Miklovich coming out and shaking hands with several senior members of the company`s staff as additional evidence."

"Mm, thanks to the steward," I added, "you may have seen the last of your Mafia top people for some time."

"I hope so," Alexei said with feeling. "Especially Leonid Davidenko. Putting him away would solve a host of problems."

CHAPTER THIRTY

I was not disappointed that the lack of snow early in the season had meant cancellation of the FIS World Cup Championships, normally held in December. I have often found that I improve as the season progresses. So, I was looking forward to the competition, particularly with the benefits of the wind tunnel identifying ways to improve my skiing style.

Todd had decided that rather than relocate the team, it would be easier to stay in Tignes, and at the start of the championships to ferry members to Val d`Isère each day. In a minibus it was no more than a twenty-minute journey between the two towns.

Moreover, he had reserved the Chalet La Face, which we would use as changing and relaxing rooms, and a large lounge area where all could gather.

What was welcome, the chalet had a spa area with indoor swimming pool and hammam. A steam bath would be ideal after a demanding day on the slopes. There was also a well-equipped room for Phyllis, our resident physio, and even a ski room with boot warmers, ensuring our kit was ready for the next day's competition.

Our performance director had chosen wisely: it was only a short distance to the `Olympique` cable car.

The Women's Super G was taking place before the men's downhill training sessions, so I spent time with her skiing on the slopes adjacent to the course before the gates were positioned. On the day of the Women's Super G, competitors were only able to assess their placement immediately prior to the event.

When the time came to make her way to the start, I watched Suzanna climb aboard the gondola, then moved close to the runout next to Todd and several others in the British team.

Todd passed his binoculars to me.

"Give them back before she's off," he declared. "I don't want you acting out her twists and turns, as you usually do, with those glued to your eyes. You'd be even more of a menace to those around you."

Although Super G is a speed event, skiers must pass through a greater number of gates, which slows them, and makes it a more technical race. As a consequence, Super G skiers have skis slightly shorter than those for the downhillers, and with more of a side cut which creates a better turning radius.

Moreover, while downhill courses start on a slope to create additional speed, Super G courses begin on a flatter plane which allows for slightly lower speeds and more focus on technique.

Suzanna was the twelfth to ski.

I handed the binoculars back to Todd with the comment. "I'm not sure I can watch this."

"Well then walk up and down, I'll call you when she's approaching the runout."

"She's skiing!" shouted Todd.

I could not help myself. I rushed to his side and peered up the course. She was flying, and I swayed through the gates with her.

"For God's sake stand still," Todd called.

Two-thirds of the way down she was a fraction of a second up on the race leader. "That's my girl!" I cried. But the lower part of the course was softer and gradually her lead slipped away to leave her in second place.

An outstanding run, and I wanted to hug her. I pushed my way through to the barrier and called out her name. Even before she removed her helmet I leaned forward and clasped her in my arms.

"Brilliant!" I shouted. "Bloody brilliant!"

Eventually, another skier edged her time, but she was on the podium in third place with a time of one minute, twenty-four point eight seconds.

The next day was the men's first downhill training session.

Instead of the Oreiller/Killy run, which ends in the outlying hamlet of La Daille, the Ski Federation had opted for the La Face de Bellevarde course, rarely raced since the World Championships in 2009.

The Face de Bellevarde is one of the more difficult runs in alpine skiing. Its high altitude is often beset with strong winds; and periodically, extreme gusts can upset a skier's line down the early part of the course.

Some skiers, who knew the course intimately, took advantage to post quick runs on the first day. However, the majority set more modest times on the three thousand metre course. I was in the latter category. Though well acquainted with the O/K course, I had never skied La

Face in competition.

For me, it was the second day of training that counted. I would go all out to make the top ten, and gain the advantage of an early run when the snow was less rutted and uneven.

Although in the past racers have complained that it was too steep, in reality La Face isn't all that bad. The top two thirds are actually quite acceptable for seasoned downhillers. It's the last thousand metres that can catch you out.

From the mountain peak there is a steep slope of more than sixty-five per cent before you face obstacles and difficult sections such as the `Bosse à Catherine` and the `Passage de L'Ancolie`, a gully between two rock walls.

On the second day of training — or practice as some skiers refer to it — I made my way up to the start accompanied by Jeff Rivers, the British Team's slalom specialist. He would take charge of my warm clothing and check my skis prior to entering the starting hut. From the gondola we joined other competitors and their helpers in the reception tent.

Eventually, it was time to transfer to the start. I slipped out of my anorak and heavyweight over-trousers, and Jeff rubbed any debris from the underside of the skis.

There were several skiers waiting to be called forward, and from their tell-tale swaying were skiing the course in their minds.

My name and number were called. I shuffled forward and lowered my poles over the wand. The beep, beep of the countdown; the starter's rhythmic flicking of fingers; and I was through the gate and pushing hard on the poles to increase speed. Two, three determined thrusts and I was flying. Easing slightly for the hairpin, side slipping on the edges to round the turn, then tucking down and propelling myself with an urgency to meet the next bend on the course.

My jumps were clean, the skis holding up as I hit another turn and rounded the gate, my body almost parallel to the hill. It`s at these moments' you don`t want to hit a rut or encounter ice that you pray the edges will hold.

Now I was on the lower part of the course, the township still far below me. I tried to increase momentum to avoid my timing drifting too far into the red zone, which meant you were losing fractions of a second behind the leader.

One last jump and I was heading for the finish line. I swept under the bridge and entered the runout. Coming to a stop I looked up at the time — three tenths of a second down on the Austrian front runner.

Taking a deep breath, I looked around for Suzanna.

I removed my skis and headed for the exit. . .and there she was.

"Wow, that was some run, Adam," she cried. "I reckon that`s more than enough for a top ten spot."

And so it was. After the last skier had completed the course, I was lying in the eighth place.

CHAPTER THIRTY-ONE

"I hear you finished inside the top ten, Adam. . .well done," Alexei remarked when I answered my mobile phone. "Tell me, are you free any time today? I wonder if we could meet? There are several things I would like to discuss with you."

I glanced at Suzanna. Today was a rest day for downhill skiers, and we were relaxing in the common room of the Chalet La Face. We had come over to Val d`Isère to support British skiers in the Men`s Giant Slalom.

"Just a moment, Alexei."

I turned to Suzanna. "It`s Alexei, could we meet him some time today?"

"Well, we should be free after three o`clock, when the competition is over."

"Alexei, we could make it at three thirty. Shall we come to your hotel?"

"Yes, that would be ideal."

The Les Barmes De l'Ours hotel was located near the ski lift, so we could call upon Sokolov on our way back to the chalet.

The door was open to his suite when we emerged from the lift.

"Come in, come in. Suzanna, it's nice to see you," he said, kissing her cheek. He turned to me, and we shook hands.

"Now, what can I get you? Wine, spirits, fruit juice?"

We both said in unison. "A cup of tea would be welcome."

He raised an eyebrow, and grinned. "You English. Of course, I forgot, it's nearly four o'clock, the time when everything stops for tea."

He picked up the phone and placed our order.

"Sit down make yourselves comfortable."

"This is a pleasant suite, Alexei," Suzanna remarked. "And what a view. You can see what's happening on the slopes without donning an anorak, winter hat, scarf, and gloves."

"Yes. . .in fact I watched Adam in the downhill yesterday. You did well, my friend."

The tea arrived, with cakes and pastries.

Alexei poured himself what looked like a whisky in a large tumbler, and sat on a settee the other side of the coffee table.

There was a brief silence while we drank our tea and nibbled at pastries.

"So, my friends, to the nub of the matter." Sokolov placed his glass on the table.

"You have done me several kindnesses. . .escorting the President's mistress back to Moscow, and identifying the involvement of the Russian Mafia in an illegal holding in a Swiss insurance company and a charitable foundation. It is now my turn.

"I have cultivated a friendship of sorts with the ship's steward. . .the one who told me of Miklovich's plans for the forthcoming Mafia gathering. For a surprisingly modest amount of Swiss Francs, he has listened in to conversations around the ship, particularly when on the bridge tuning in to conversations by the captain and the senior members of the crew. As a consequence, he has given me almost a complete itinerary, when in twenty-four hours' time, the Russian Mafia hierarchy descend upon Lucerne.

"Apparently, they will board the Stadt Luzern paddle steamer with the notion of enjoying a good lunch, before being presented with the latest details of their vast profits from their rackets, drug trafficking, prostitution, and gambling operations. The session will be led by Boris Miklovich, their finance man. There is little doubt he will also reveal the results of their prized possessions, `Die Versicherungs Gesellschaft der Luzern and the Unterstützungsfond Für Professional Skiläufer`."

Sokolov picked up his glass and drank deeply before continuing.

I studied Alexei's face. "You're aiming to catch them red-handed, aren't you. I'll bet you've already informed the Swiss authorities of their illegal activities concerning the insurance company and the Professional Skiers Charity Fund, and the police will be waiting on the quay to arrest them. That right, Alexei?"

"Better than that, Adam, they'll be on the ship, posing as stewards, waiters and crew members. I've discussed what we want to do with the company owning the vessel, and they are keen to help. So, when we have recorded much of what Miklovich has to say, the Bratva top brass will be arrested. The ship returns to the quayside where police vehicles will be waiting to carry them off to jail. . .and I`m going to be there to witness it!"

"Alexei, that`s brilliant," declared Suzanna. "Many Russians will now sleep more soundly in their beds. I`ll bet your boss is pleased. Earlier, you mentioned it was now your turn. What did you mean by that?"

Sokolov nodded. "Simply this, Suzanna. When we take Miklovich into custody, firstly, he won`t be in a position to fulfil his side of the contract on you by paying his hired help; and secondly, I`ll get the police to pressurise Miklovich into revealing the name of his hit man. That`s the least they can do after giving them the Mafia hierarchy on a plate. Then we can take action to neutralise him, or them. So, you should soon be in the clear."

"Thank God for that," Suzanna breathed a sigh of relief. "So we`ll only need your minder for a little while longer. Mind you, Alexei, we haven`t seen hide nor hair of him these past weeks. Are you sure he is still dogging our footsteps; we have been travelling to a good many places?"

Sokolov looked hesitant. "Truth to tell, Suzanna, I have not been able to contact him. In fact, I`ve lost track of him since you returned from America."

"Alexei, as a matter of interest, what does your man look like?" I asked. "Just in case we spot him."

Alexei nodded. "I doubt you`ll spot him. He is quite tall, and has a narrow build, which makes him appear even taller. He`s in his late thirties."

I glanced at Suzanna, but she had not made the connection. The man who stepped out of the shadows in Aspen was tall, and wearing a hat, which shadowed his face. Had Josh Finden accidentally shot our minder in the belief he was a mugger? Uncertain of the possible error I said nothing to Alexei.

CHAPTER THIRTY-TWO

Race day once again.

Much to Suzanna`s amusement I go through a series of exercises when preparing to race. The first ritual is to lie in a hot bath, then slowly reduce the water temperature until it is really cold.

Then a brisk rub-down with towels. After that a host of bending and stretching movements followed by a slice of toast and tea. Nothing else. I cannot eat a meal prior to skiing in competition.

She watched me go through my routine, all the while grinning while sitting up in bed eating a hearty breakfast. After that I usually sleep for a couple of hours until it is time to gather my equipment and don my catsuit.

"Do you want a hand getting into that?" Suzanna asked guilelessly, though I knew she was secretly laughing at me as I rolled around the floor pulling on the tight-fitting all-in-one suit.

"No," I said curtly, puffing at my exertions.

The morning slipped by. Then it was time to take the gondola up to the top of the Bellevarde. The number nine on my bib indicated my place in the starting line-up.

It seemed to come round almost too quickly.

I stayed briefly in the reception tent; and when called forward, I shuffled into the start hut with Todd by my side. There were two skiers in front of me. There was no interruption and what seemed like seconds later I took my place by the starter. Poles over the wand, I adopted the familiar crouch with my arms slightly bent for maximum leverage.

Then the countdown, my eyes fixed on the steep slope before me.

With one almighty heave I broke the wand and used my poles, once, twice, three times to gain speed.

Off the gradient I turned into the first bend, hard on the edges to side slip through the gate. My skis hit ice, but not enough to take me off course. Through the Bosse à Catherine I took off with a jump of about forty metres. Another turn, this time to the right. Better, no ice this time. In the tuck I remembered to hold my arms tighter to my body, as suggested by the people operating the wind tunnel.

Coming up fast, the Bec de l'Aigle — the Eagle's Beak — a hairpin bend. Once more, almost lying parallel to the snow, I relied on my edges to take me through the gate.

Next, the Grand Mur, followed quickly by the Buse. My legs were feeling the strain of holding a tuck position and the demands of sideslipping to grab the best line down the course. Now I was building up speed, heading for the Passage de L`Ancolie. The surface through the eight-metre-wide gap between two rock formations is icy and I concentrate hard on keeping my skis from slipping.

My breathing is short, and I`m panting as the vista of

Val d'Isère appears almost beneath my feet. In a course length of three thousand metres, I've dropped a thousand metres, and once more I'm accelerating towards the finish. The pain is hard to bear, but I force myself into a tuck approaching the Bosse à Cathiard, a series of bumps that lead to another jump of fifty metres.

The finish line flashes by, and I side-slip to a halt in the runout.

All I want to do is sink to the ground. I lean on my poles in exhaustion.

Then I hear Suzanna's voice. She is shouting something.

I slowly stand erect, take off my helmet and lean to her across the barrier. We bang heads as we kiss.

She breaks free, and tells me the time. "Adam, you did two minutes, seven point two six seconds. You're in first place!

Of course it did not last.

The next racer is on his way, and the split time already shows he is quicker over the initial section to the Grand Mur. I wipe a glove across my face. Light snow is falling, the light is fading.

The skier crosses the line; but he has lost time on the final section, putting him half a second behind me.

Next to come is Ivan Müller of Germany, the fastest man during the preliminaries. The snow is falling more heavily, but the top of the run is still unaffected, and Müller is close to a second up.

He loses some of that margin on the bottom slopes, but on the line the scoreboard shows him five hundredths of a second faster, and I vacate the leader's stand in favour of the German.

As the snowfall moves up the mountain most of the other racers record slower times; until Lavinsky of Poland enjoys a brief window when the clouds roll back, the snowfall clears, the light improves.

The conditions suit the Pole, and by the merest fraction he manages to grab second place. Nevertheless, I was delighted with a podium finish.

Todd was highly complementary back at the Chalet La Face.

"How about that everybody. . .two British skiers coming in third in their disciplines! What a result. . .what could be better."

There was cheering and whistling from team members, and we drank to Suzanna's and my success with cups of tea.

"Actually," I said to the room, "the results were down to Todd. It was he who suggested Suzanna and I might benefit from using a wind tunnel. He was right. Suzanna needed to improve her stance leaving the gate, and I should keep my elbows tighter to my body, especially in the tuck position, Doing so meant gaining valuable fractions of a second. So, Todd, thank you."

Another group cheer. Todd smiled deprecatingly.

Suzanna turned to me. "Now the Championships are finished would you come with me tomorrow morning and ski La Face course from the top? The Super G run is only half the hill. I'd like to experience the whole three thousand metres."

"Of course. . .Though we'll have to take it carefully. By now the gates have been removed and the safety netting taken down. It`s open now to the general public."

"In which case we`ll go early. I`ll speak with Todd for the minibus to take us."

Back in Tignes Suzanna and I made love with a tender commitment I did not think possible. I was more exhausted than when I finished the downhill a couple of hours earlier.

Lying entwined I was totally relaxed, almost in a stupor when my cell phone rang. In a tangle of arms and legs I failed to reach it before it rang off.

"Leave it," murmured Suzanna. "Whoever it is will try again."

But whoever it was, I had a feeling it was important, a premonition that I should be concerned. I eased myself from the bed and padded across to the phone on the coffee table.

It was Alexei Sokolov`s number and he had left a message.

`Adam listen carefully. I could well be wrong you will soon be in the clear. Our operation in Lucerne went well. However, interrogating Miklovich, before the police hauled him off to jail, he was surprisingly forthcoming. Probably, knowing the game was up and get a lighter sentence, he revealed much of what the Bratva is up to currently.

`He even mentioned Vasiliev seeing him in Lucerne, and making the connection between the insurance company and the skiers` charity. One thing he added, he`ll try to stop the contract out on you and Suzanna. I gave him my phone to make contact with his hired assassin, but he couldn`t reach him, though he tried several times.

`I`m leaving Lucerne and will be come straight to Val d`Isère. In the meantime, stay in your room as much as possible, and if you leave it make sure you are both with a crowd. See you soon."

I took the cell phone to the bed and handed it to Suzanna.

"Listen to this. It might be critical, something Sokolov feels we ought to heed."

A minute later, her face turned ashen. "My God, do you think whoever is out there, is still after us?"

"There are several possibilities." I said thoughtfully. "One, it might be a product of Alexei`s fevered imagination. Two, Miklovich could be looking to improve his bargaining stance by building up the drama if he appears not to reach his so-called contractor. Or three, like Sokolov said earlier, our would-be assassin is no longer interested because the money supply has been cut off."

"What do you really believe? What shall we do?"

"Either way, for the moment we heed Alexei`s advice," I replied. "We were talking about skiing La Face early tomorrow morning, do you still want to go, or shall we scotch the idea?"

Suzanna gnawed at her bottom lip. Then she made up her mind. "Dammit. . .I`m not going to be prisoner to my own concerns We go. . . the earlier the better. That way who in their right mind would be out on the slopes waiting to get us?"

Just before we went down for dinner there was a knock on the door.

Suzanna looked up wide-eyed. "Do we answer that?" she whispered.

"I`ll check who it is," I murmured.

I squinted through the spyhole.

"It`s OK, it`s only Josh Finden," I said in a normal voice, opening the door. "Come in, Josh. It`s good to see you."

As he walked past me he hesitated at seeing Suzanna.

"Adam, the reason I came was to discuss where and when you`ll be skiing next season. As we normally do about this time, we should discuss your thoughts before I get my team to make all the arrangements. I`ve got the dates of the various competitions, and a list of likely sponsors. Coming third in today`s big event lifts your stock even higher. What it now needs is your agreement to the events and, of course, signatures on the usual contract."

"Well, I don`t think I can discuss it right now, Josh. But what about tomorrow morning? Suzanna and I are going for an early morning run on the downhill course, so could we make eleven o`clock in the hotel lounge?"

"No problem at all. Eleven o`clock it is. Do you have an agent, Suzanna?" Josh enquired.

"I don`t think I need one yet. Perhaps when I`ve moved further up the rankings," she replied crisply.

Josh smiled and nodded. "When you`re ready, my dear, I`ll be only too pleased to have you on our books."

As the lift doors opened to take us down three flights, Suzanna muttered. "It`s odd, Adam, but I don`t feel comfortable with your agent."

"Why ever not? He has always done well by me."

With others in the lift the topic was dropped.

CHAPTER THIRTY-THREE

When the minibus came to a halt by the ski lift, we were the only people taking a gondola up the Bellevarde.

At the top the reception tent and the starting hut were still to be dismantled; but, as I expected, the gate flags had been removed; and the safety netting lining the course now rolled into bundles ready to be put in store.

The blue guidelines, indicating the course, would disappear with the next snowfall. However, this morning we would follow their meandering path down to the township.

We were adjusting our skis, securing zips, and slipping on gloves when Suzanna looked up and froze. What had she seen?

I turned round to see a figure emerge from the reception tent.

I was puzzled. . .what was he doing up here?

"I thought we were meeting at eleven, Josh. We`re just about to ski down La Face."

"I don`t think so, Adam." As he spoke, his right hand drew a weapon from a pocket. "What better place to finish what I`ve been attempting to do the past weeks."

"What are you talking about?"

"Don't you know?" He glanced at Suzanna. "I'll bet she does. Don't you?" He pointed the gun at her and I started forward, but he quickly aimed at me.

"Stay where you are," he snarled. Then his voice changed to almost to a purr. "So who's going to be first. You decide. . .or shall I decide for you? Either way, I shall be the only one riding the mountain."

"Who's behind this, Finden? If it's the Bratva you should know that Miklovich is now in jail, along with many others."

He sneered at me. "I know, and you probably helped bring him down. But you see, it's a question of reputation. I cannot be seen failing to complete a contract. To do so reduces my worth to likely sponsors."

He hefted the gun in his hand. "OK, enough said. . .you're first, Suzanna."

Suzanna moved towards Finden in supplication, her face twisted in anguish.

"Oh, please, Mr Finden, I don't want to die. Just shoot Adam. After all he was your target. I won't say a word, I promise." She moved further towards him.

Josh's gun hand wavered, and then started turning towards me, when Suzanna swung her right leg, the ski caught Finden's elbow, and the automatic pirouetted into the air landing four or five metres away.

Then she kicked him in the groin, shouting. "Now, Adam, ski for our lives!"

We started down the Petit Col, no gentle side to side descent, but a full-blooded straight line, with all the speed we could muster. Finden had retrieved the gun, looking back I could see he was now in pursuit.

"I'll go first, Suzanna," I shouted. "I know the best line through the turns."

I swung into the first bend, and hit ice. Fortunately, it was patchy and I managed to hold the slight slip of my left ski.

"Careful," I called over my shoulder. "It`s icy!"

Through the Bosse à Catherine.

"Jump coming up," I yelled.

We soared together landing with little difficulty thirty metres on.

Then the Bec de l'Aigle, and back on our edges.

Glancing back, Finden was still some seventy or eighty metres behind us.

Suzanna is an accomplished skier, but the men`s downhill course is demanding and I realised she was beginning to tire. We might not make it to safety before Finden closed on us.

We were fast approaching the Passage de L`Ancolie, where the course narrows between two rock formations. As we swept into the gap I side-slipped to a halt. Suzanna stopped further down.

"What the hell are you doing?" she yelled.

"Don`t stop! Go on! Go on!"

"No way. If you stop, so do I!"

I started dragging bundles of safety netting across the path through the rocks. Quickly realising what I was up to Suzanna also began pulling the netting across the snow.

Just seconds before our would-be killer swept into the passage.

Josh saw us waiting by the exit, then the netting in his path.

He may once have been a very capable skier, but time had robbed him of the ability to jump and clear even modest obstacles. He skied towards the one small gap remaining, but it was his undoing.

He was too close to the wall. A protruding rock caught his arm, swinging him round. Like a marionette with broken strings, he was buffeted unmercifully by the unforgiving granite. His body careered down the slope at increasing widening angles.

"Stay there," I said to Suzanna, and skied slowly to where Josh Finden lay. It was evident he was mortally injured as the snow reddened beneath him.

"So I failed to complete the contract after all," he whispered, grimacing with the pain.

I knelt beside him.

"Josh, did you fulfil a contract on Anatoly Vasiliev?"

With effort, he nodded his head.

"And Ron Grainger?"

Again he nodded, but his eyes were dimming.

"And our protector in Aspen?"

"No, he wasn't your protector," he gasped with his dying breath.

I made my way up the slope.

Suzanna had already dragged the netting back to the side.

From the Chalet La Face we phoned the police and reported the accident.

An hour later two officers interviewed Suzanna and I, and took our statements. The tone of both our responses was we had met Josh Finden, a sports agent, on the peak of Bellevarde. We were skiing down La Face together, when he accelerated through the Ancolie passage and mis-judged his line on the early morning ice. The consequences were fatal.

The officers accepted our comments, for they matched the abrasion marks on the rock wall, and the bloody trail down to where his body had come to rest. Moreover, the attendant at the ski lift remembered us travelling alone.

We met Alexei Sokolov at the Ferme des Capucines, a restaurant housed in an authentic Savoyard farmhouse on the outskirts of Tignes.

As usual, Alexei was there before us, and had already drunk much of the bottle of white wine on the table.

"Come sit with me, my friends. Waiter, another bottle of Roussanne," he called. "You`ll like this," he said. "It`s a local wine with plenty of body."

The bottle appeared, and was poured into our glasses.

"So," continued Alexei, "both coming third deserves a toast. I salute you." He raised his glass and tilted it in our direction. "Now, let me tell you about Lucerne. It went so well, I can hardly believe it. In fact, I`m still wondering why the Bratva hierarchy didn`t catch onto the possibility they could be rounded up like fish in a net.

"Apparently, Miklovich had convinced them that sailing the lake in a paddle steamer with only them on board would provide all the security they needed. On the water they could talk freely without fear their innermost secrets could be overheard. Were they in for a surprise!

"After a light lunch they assembled in the upper salon, and Leonid Davidenko officially welcomed them all to the financial review. Boris Miklovich then led them through all their money-making activities, including their insurance company, and the skiers` benevolent fund.

"What I didn`t realise was how they manipulated their co-existence. The insurance company was an active sponsor, a benefactor which gave regularly to the fund; and just as frequently, the fund invested in the insurance company. A sure-fire way to launder money, and the Swiss were none the wiser, until they heard it for themselves."

"So you recorded the review then?" Suzanna enquired.

Alexei smiled. "Not only that we filmed it as well!"

"Well done, Alexei," I raised my glass. "You've pulled off quite a coup."

"You wouldn't believe how important it was."

Then, as though an after-thought, he said. "By the way, I've spoken with my man. Protection for both of you will be instigated for first thing tomorrow morning."

"There's no need, Alexei," Suzanna urbanely remarked. "Adam and I have already dealt with the matter."

His brow furrowed. "What do you mean, 'dealt with the matter'?"

She glanced at me, as though asking, shall I tell him, or will you?

"Go ahead," I said.

"We have to go back to Bischofshofen, when Anatoly Vasiliev was jumping for the Four Hills title. He was way ahead of the others, and needed, for him, only a modest jump to take the trophy. You know what happened, and it was all due to one man. . Josh Finden. It was he, or rather his technical specialist, Ron Grainger. Mixing with other technicians when setting up the skis, no one would notice Grainger doctoring Vasiliev's binding. And it happened, as you now know, because Vasiliev saw and checked Boris Miklovich's involvement in The Lucerne Insurance Company and the Professional Skiers' Benevolent Fund.

"And it snowballed to include Adam," declared Suzanna. "The Russian Mafia could not ignore the possibility that Anatoly told Adam, so he had to be dealt with. Fortunately for him," she grabbed my hand, as tears welled up in her eyes. "Fortunately for him, lady luck and good fortune spoiled several attempts to rid the world of my man."

She released my hand while she searched her bag for a tissue. Then added. "The penultimate attempt was in Aspen."

"Penultimate?" queried Alexei. "Do you mean there was another?"

"Earlier this morning, Alexei. But let me talk about Aspen. For some reason, Finden was in Aspen when Adam believed he was in Europe. He appeared suddenly when we had just left a party, and were on our way back to the hotel. We now realise that he intended to gun down Adam and I when your protector came out the shadows to save us from Josh Finden.

"In trying to get a clearer view of our would-be assassin, your man left it just a fraction too late, Finden shot him. At the time we thought he had saved us from being mugged, whereas your minder was trying to protect Adam and myself. I`m so sorry, Alexei."

Alexei was silent for a moment.

"I never knew that, Suzanna. He had disappeared off the radar."

"No. . .as Suzanna has said, we thought he was a notorious mugger,"

I explained. "And Josh Finden had done the authorities a good turn by removing him. I`m sorry, Alexei, if he were our protector, he died safeguarding Suzanna and I."

The Russian shook his head at the revelation. Then he asked. "So, what happened this morning?"

I took up the story.

"Last night when we were getting ready for dinner, Josh Finden knocked on our door. As my agent, he wanted to discuss the coming season's activities . . . what competitions, sponsorships, equipment, so his people could start planning and making the bookings. I said we could meet today at eleven o'clock, after Suzanna and I had skied the downhill course before others were about. I didn't realise I was playing into his hands.

"Today, we took an early gondola to the peak, and were preparing for the run, when he came out the reception tent brandishing a gun. You were right when you said we would still be pursued, even if the people behind the whole affair could no longer support the contract. To Finden it was a matter of honour, of saving his reputation. At that point he was intent on fulfilling the task, having been thwarted on several previous occasions."

I looked at Suzanna. "It was a frightening moment. We were alone on the mountain with a psychopath. Cleverly, Suzanna played a terrified soul, and whined that he should shoot me, she wanted nothing to do with me. All the while she was getting closer to him. Sufficiently close, to kick the gun from his hand with her ski.

Then we took off down the course with all the speed we could muster. Retrieving his gun Finden set off after us. Some years ago, he too, had been a downhiller."

"The turning point was when we skied through the Passage de L'Ancolie," Suzanna declared. "Adam and I stopped and threw bundles of safety netting into the passage. Finden saw the netting and veered towards a gap close to the rocks. He misjudged the outcrop, which was his undoing. He hit the rock wall and suffered fatal injuries as he tumbled down the slope."

"My God, what an experience," Sokolov said quietly.

What we had recounted had the effect of sobering Alexei Sokolov. The rest of the meal, the rest of the evening, he was quite subdued until he was despatched in a taxi to his hotel in Val d'Isère.

We walked back to the Résidence Bonhomme Neige holding hands. I savoured the moment we were free from the wiles of Bratva`s killer. A distinctly rosy future lay ahead.

Or so I thought.

CHAPTER THIRTY-FOUR

There's no easy way to get to the Grandvalira region of Andorra.

Making the journey by road was the best option. However, it was over seven hundred and fifty kilometres from Tignes to Soldeu, where the International Ski Federation Finals were being held.

It took close to eight hours in the coach. Although we stopped at a Brioche Dorée on the outskirts of Nîmes to stretch our legs and for something to eat.

Suzanna, of course, fell asleep shortly after leaving Tignes, and only blearily awoke when the coach came to a halt. She had been oblivious to the tedium everyone else had endured for the past four hours.

"Where are we?" were her first words.

"Somewhere near Nîmes, I think," I replied, as she lifted her head from my shoulder, and sat upright.

"Really? Are you sure? I only dozed off for a short while."

Suzanna leaned forward and put her head in the gap between the seats.

"Lisa, do you know where we are?"

"Haven't a clue, though I guess we are still in France,"

came Lisa's reply.

"We don't want to be too long everybody," called Todd, standing by the driver at the front of the coach. "Let's be on the road again in thirty minutes."

I don't remember much of the next part of the journey, for I, too, fell asleep. Eventually, jaded, weary and in need of a shower, we arrived at the Sports Hotel Village in the centre of the town.

I had not been to Soldeu before, nor skied on any of the Grandvalira slopes. So the region and the downhill course would be a new experience.

Entering the hotel, I was struck by the atrium, which was all wood panelling beams, and the rich smell of pine; and this theme was carried throughout the hotel, even in the bedrooms.

Our spacious room was on the fourth floor, with a magnificent view of the mountainside. Moreover, the hotel's location was ideal for the Slalom and Giant Slalom competitors, for it was only a few steps to the ski lift up the Avet slopes.

The Super G and the Downhill would be held further along the valley on the Aliga slopes. The start, reached by ski lift or gondola, was from the nearby village of El Tarter. Because of the hilly terrain, El Tarter was three kilometres from Soldeu by road. The straight-line distance, less than a kilometre.

According to the number of points gained during the skiing season, the top twenty-five skiers from each discipline compete for the International Ski Federation's annual award. Last year's winner was leading the Downhill standings with five hundred points, and only a skier from Switzerland, with four hundred and sixty points, could take the trophy, if he raced to victory in the Downhill in three days' time.

I had no chance of even being in the first twenty places. I had not competed or excelled in a sufficient number of races to be anywhere close to the leaders. However, I would do my damnedest to feature in the top five in the last downhill race of the season.

Suzanna lay on the bed, while I stood before the full-length window gazing up the slopes where the Slaloms would be held. Suddenly, there was a knock on the door. Suspicious of any incident out of the norm, I peered intently through the spyhole in the door.

"It's Greg Nichols," I murmured over my shoulder. "Now, what's he doing here?"

I opened the door, looked up and down the corridor, and beckoned him in.

"Sorry, if I disturbed you," he said, more to Suzanna than to me.

She smiled, but did not move, other to raise a hand.

"Hello, Adam, I was just checking to make sure the British contingent had arrived."

Then, with the next breath, he said. "Would you care to dine with me tonight. I've already discovered the food here is pretty good."

I must admit I hesitated, but Suzanna jumped off the bed and said, "What a good idea, Greg. We haven't seen you for a while, we'd love to. What time. . .eight o'clock in the restaurant? That will give us time to relax and have a shower."

"Excellent, well I won`t keep you. . .see you both at eight." And he was gone.

"You were going to say no, weren`t you," remarked Suzanna.

"Quite frankly, yes. How did you know?"

"I`m getting to know your ways, my lad," she replied. Then added with a faint lift of an eyebrow. "I told him we would relax for a while after a journey. . .so that`s what we are going to do. Come on you," she declared, pulling me down onto the bed.

There was little time thereafter to relax.

Suzanna and I were walking towards the restaurant, when I voiced a thought that had been on my mind. "Why do you think he was so keen to dine with us tonight?"

"I was wondering that as well. Perhaps he wants your advice on a new agent, now Josh Finden is no longer with us."

"That could be it, I suppose."

As we threaded our way through the tables, Greg rose to his feet and formally shook hands with Suzanna and me. We sat either side of him, where there were already filled glasses.

"I have taken the liberty of ordering aperitifs. I wanted you to join me in drinking this delicious Kirsch. It comes from fermented, double-distilled cherry juice."

I tasted mine, and had to agree, it was delicious. Moreover, our glasses were quickly refilled. It was only later I realised it as an attempt to soften the impact of what our host was about to say.

At first there was a mutual silence while we examined

the menu. Minds made up; a waiter took our orders. Greg summoned the sommelier and reserved several bottles of wine for the meal.

An expectant air enveloped Suzanna and I.

Neither of us spoke. I stared reflectively into my glass of kirsch; she studied the wine list on the table.

"I suppose you are wondering why I asked you to dine with me," Greg said, breaking the silence. "I guess an explanation is required. Really, I should not be telling you this, but I have been speaking with my good friend, Alexei Sokolov, who assures me that I can trust you. Let me begin by saying I am a Canadian citizen, known as Gregory Nichols. However, I am also Grigory Nikolaev, and I work for the Federal'naya Sluzhba Bezopasnosti..."

"The what?" I interrupted.

"The Russian Federal Security Service, darling," remarked Suzanna. "The FSB."

Greg hesitated, then the words tumbled out. "I'm not a full-time operative, you understand, just called upon when required. There are a good many people like me in the world, employed by the FSB to do courier, surveillance, and occasionally protection work."

"So you were our protector, were you?" asked Suzanna.

"Yes, Alexei asked me to undertake the task of keeping you safe."

"But you were around long before Alexei called upon your services," I reminded him.

"True...you see I'm also a skier, my speciality is the slalom. I am hoping to make the Canadian team. However, I was told to get myself involved with the Finden Ski School, so they could coach me to become a downhiller. I was given a handsome sum of money to persuade Josh Finden to take me on as my agent, and for the school to guide me through the art of skiing downhill."

"The real reason being?" questioned Suzanna.

"To discover if the ski instructors in his company were involved in drug trafficking on behalf of Bratva. Let me explain."

"We know what the Bratva is, unfortunately," I said grimly. "Josh Finden was undoubtedly close to Miklovich, and it now looks as though Finden was their tame assassin."

"I wonder if he had accomplices, "Suzanna remarked . "Josh could not have contrived all the so-called accidents on his own." Then, as an afterthought, she added. "Who else was with Finden when he had a gun in Aspen?"

Nichols stroked his chin. "On reflection, I believe there was someone with him, or standing nearby. At the time who it was didn`t register."

"Well, we know for certain Ron Grainger, Finden`s technician, was sabotaging the skis," Suzanna declared. "That`s one of them. . . I`m sure there were others."

"Thinking back to Aspen," said Nichols, "I was at the crud party, but it was so crowded I didn`t see you leave, otherwise I would have followed you."

"Which suggests," Suzanna said thoughtfully, "that the fellow shot by Finden really was a mugger."

"I think so. When I noticed you weren`t there, I went to the entrance to check if you were outside," Greg explained, "just as Finden was raising his gun. Possibly to shoot you as well. He must have seen me and thought better of it."

"Tell me, Greg, or Grigory, when did Alexei ask you

to keep an eye on us?" Suzanna enquired.

"In Rosa Khutor. I was still checking Finden's people, not making much headway, when Alexei asked me to keep a close watch on you two. Although, the major players of the Bratva are now behind bars, I've continued to act as your discreet protector. According to Alexei, there is still the possibility someone else might make an attempt on your lives.

"When everyone moved on to Aspen, I followed. I knew you would be safe in a crowd before I arrived twelve hours later. After that, I mixed with the British contingent, spent time with Finden's people, and everywhere you went I was close. Like you, having been told he was in Italy, I was also surprised to see Josh Finden in Aspen that night."

"Well, he's out of the way now," I remarked. "So I don't see the likelihood we'll be the target for anyone else."

"Look, Alexei believes you are still in danger," Greg said flatly. "He wants me to be even closer to you. As a consequence, I wanted to let you know what I was about in case you thought me some kind of stalker. Like Alexei, I believe anything could happen."

CHAPTER THIRTY-FIVE

With two days to go before the first round of training, I was anxious to get onto the Grandvalira slopes. New to Soldeu I needed to be conversant with the jumps, the twists and turns of the downhill before the competition started.

Until the hill was closed to the public, I would have to moderate my speed, but that was not a problem. I would be stopping frequently to assess the most favourable line down the course.

Suzanna was still in bed when I went down to the lobby and met up with Nichols.

"What do I call you? Is it still Greg, or would you now prefer Grigory?" I asked as we wandered out the hotel entrance and beckoned a taxi.

Stowing our skis on the roof rack we climbed into the back seats.

"Greg. . .I`m more comfortable with that," he murmured.

In El Tarter the taxi turned off the main road, and immediately encountered drifting snow. The driver carried on, but taking us across the river bridge was a struggle. After another hundred metres, it was obvious he could go no further. I paid for the brief ride and removed our skis from the roof rack. We were about to walk to the gondola station when, of all people, Lars Oestensson appeared.

"The queue for gondolas is horrendous," he exclaimed. "I'm told it would make more sense to take the chair lift. I'm off there now, why don't you join me?"

"What are you doing here, Lars?" Greg asked. "This is not Nordic country."

"I was invited by the Nordic Ski Club in Colomiers, just outside Toulouse, to give advice about the demands of the Biathlon. You need to build up body strength and your stamina to ski long distances, stopping briefly to shoot at targets. Afterwards, being close to Soldeu, I thought I'd come and support my home nation in the alpine events."

We skied through a sudden snowfall that added several centimetres to the already thick carpet, completely obliterating where the road might be.

There were few skiers about. The squally weather, and the rapid build-up of snow were clearly dissuading many from venturing out at this early hour.

"Just a moment," called Lars, "I need something from my bag."

We halted while he put down the holdall and tugged at the zip. He had his back to us. I turned to look at the ski lift station. Even from a distance it was evident it was not inundated with skiers.

"What the hell!" I heard Greg shout.

I looked back to see Oestensson pointing his competition rifle at us.

"I remember now," said Greg calmly. "You were the one in Aspen, standing in Finden's shadow."

"Why did you have to poke your nose in our business," Lars snarled. "Josh was about to take out Livesey when you appeared, damn you! So, for being a nuisance you can join him."

With the touch of a finger, he slotted a round into the breech. I looked over his shoulder.

"So you were Josh Finden`s hired help," I said, hoping he would revel in the situation, albeit it briefly, "I should have realised. What Suzanna saw in you I can`t begin to imagine."

He grinned sardonically.

"She was about to fall for my charms, Livesey. You would have lost her to me if she hadn`t felt compassion for your injuries. But, after I`ve dealt with you two, I`ll take my pleasures with her, before she, too, is despatched."

I was desperate to keep him talking.

Greg realised why.

"Do you honestly believe Suzanna will fall for your line in seduction?" I remarked.

Oestensson grinned at me and swung the rifle to point at my chest. "She will when I break the news of your death. I shall comfort her, then, oh so gradually, use her favours. She will be like putty in my hands."

I was seething with rage. It was all I could do to stop myself charging at him, regardless of the weapon trained on me. After all a .22 bullet can do little extensive damage.

He must have caught the briefest flash of anger.

"I am not using competition rounds. These," he tapped his weapon fondly. "I`ve loaded a heavier, longer bullet that will snuff you out like blowing on a candle."

I shrugged. "Even if I die today Suzanna will easily

resist your advances. She is made of sterner stuff."

"It`s a pity you won`t be around to witness how easily she will fall into my arms. Now, say a silent prayer." He changed the angle slightly, pointing the rifle at my head.

"Hello! Is the chair lift working?"

The question was posed by one of six skiers making their way towards the lift station. Coming up behind Oesstensson, he had been unaware of their presence while I had kept him talking.

"Yes it`s working. Our friend here was just showing us his biathlon competition rifle. Better put it away, Lars."

Oestensson was caught out. He should have used his rifle when the opportunity first existed. Encouraging him to crow about his manly charms had ruined the attempt. His couldn`t shoot everyone. Another opportunity missed; and his face displayed his mounting anger. The odds had changed. . .if only slightly.

We joined the group and continued towards the chairlift station. As we got closer, my mind was racing, how do we get out of this situation?

A thought popped into my head. I suddenly remembered the evening when we were all dining together. Looking directly at Suzanna, Oestensson had suggested a nightcap before retiring, and she had joined him.

As I made for the lifts, Josh Finden had remarked. "I`d watch out, Adam, Lars is a fast worker."

I had not thought about the comment until this moment; but analysing it now, it was obvious Finden and Oestensson had known one another for some time.

"Be ready, Greg. When I say now," I murmured, "just follow me, OK?"

He nodded. I could see Oestensson tense as we approached the station.

"Now!" I shouted and skied around the barrier, ahead of the group waiting for the gate to release.

There were shouts of irritation as the chair came round and we dropped onto the seat. They rose even louder when Lars commandeered the next chair.

"We could be in trouble," I said to Greg, as I looked back to see Oestensson calmly removing the rifle from his carry-bag and checking the sights before reloading.

We were moving steadily up the mountainside, when the first bullet thumped into the back of the seat.

"Christ! We`re sitting targets," cried Nichols. "Get down low. Pray he is a better skier than a marksman!"

Although the back rest was low, the chair was designed to carry four people, so we were able to lie low across the bench seat.

I had been carrying my helmet, gloves, and goggles in a backpack. I twisted out of the straps, removed the helmet, and stuck it on my head.

A bullet thudded into the back rest. Then another, ten or fifteen seconds later.

"He`s playing with us," groaned Nichols.

As he bent low his anorak gaped, and I saw what appeared to be the grip of a handgun in an inside pocket.

There seemed to be a lull in the firing.

Greg tentatively raised his head above the chair back.

I was not sure where the bullet hit him. It happened too quickly. Greg was already toppling sideways when I heard the crack of Lars` rifle.

In slow motion Greg slipped under the safety bar and fell from the chair. Looking down we were a good twenty metres above the rising terrain, and almost halfway up the mountainside. If the bullet did not take him out, the fall most surely would.

There was nothing I could do. The barrage continued, and the chair where I was crouching was gradually falling to pieces every time a bullet embedded itself into the fabric of the chair back.

Suddenly, my backpack suffered a hit. It would not withstand the onslaught like the chair. Any time now, a bullet was going to pass through the pack and strike home.

The upper station was getting closer. Time to act. . .but how could I escape Lars` shooting me down like a hunter after game. Two metres from the ground I pushed up the bar and leapt out the chair lift. Jumping in downhill racing you often reach such heights. Though the landing is more a glide, not a sharp, downwards impact. The jolt winded me, but I dared not stop. A quick turn and I was off down the slope, momentarily confusing Oestensson.

But he was soon after me. Brushing aside those who had witnessed him shooting at us.

I had a fifty-metre head start as I skied to the spot where Greg`s body should be. With my life in jeopardy this was not the time to fall, or falter in any way. I urged myself on, not looking over my shoulder to see if Lars were closing the gap. I slowed, desperately casting around. I was sure this was the location. But he was nowhere to be seen.

I headed for a deep drift of snow.

This could be my last hope.

And there he was, lying on his back, about half a metre down.

As I waded into the drift, I could hear the swish of approaching skis. This was no time for gently prising open Greg`s anorak. I tore at the zip, and plunged my hand into the pocket.

Thank God. . .it was a gun.

"There you are! Hiding from me were you!" His voice had a contemptuous ring. "Well, lie there for all I care. . .it can be your grave." He laughed. "No one will find you until the Spring!"

I slowly eased the automatic from the pocket, the other hand hiding the removal.

"Don`t forget the safety catch," Greg murmured.

Jesus! A voice from the grave.

"While I`m at it, I`ll shoot Nichols to be absolutely sure."

They were the last words Lars spoke.

As he was priming his rifle, I swung round, and more by luck than judgement, fired the gun. It slammed into Oestensson, creating a neat, round hole in his forehead and blowing off the back of his head.

The look of surprise was still on his face when the authorities came to view and remove the body. Greg Nichols was airlifted to hospital, suffering two broken legs and a bullet furrow along the right-hand side of his skull.

I never did ski in the Soldeu Downhill.

While Greg Nichols was in the local hospital under the watchful eye of a police officer, I was remanded for questioning, and missed the training sessions on the Aliga slopes.

The interrogation by the police was unrelenting. However, after so many witnesses came forward to give their versions of the incident, the authorities decided I was more the victim than the executioner.

They could understand Oestensson having the competition rifle, but how did I come by the automatic pistol? I had to reveal I had taken it from the pocket of Grigory Nikolaev, a Russian diplomat.

When Suzanna and I visited Greg, I apologised for revealing how I had come by the weapon.

"Do not apologise, my friend. They questioned me, too. I simply told them the Bratva had a contract out on me, and when I visited our embassy in Madrid the gun was issued to me. As you well know their hitman almost got me on two occasions. In the chair lift, and then lying helpless in the snow. It was a good thing, I said, that Adam Livesey was there, and used the weapon to protect me."

On the second visit to the hospital Greg had another visitor. Alexei Sokolov was sitting in a bedside chair. He rose quickly and gave me the Russian equivalent of a bear hug. Rewarding, but painful.

"Adam, my dear, dear friend!" he said smiling. "It looks like that`s the end of it all. A few bruises, but you live to tell the tale, eh!"

"More than just a few bruises, Alexei. But that`s how I met Suzanna, so I cannot complain."

"By the way, where is she?"

"About to compete in the Women`s Super G, so this is just a brief visit to see if Greg wanted anything."

"Not at the moment, Adam," he replied. But thank you."

I reached out and shook his hand.

"We may well meet again, Alexei. Just give me warning where you`ll be skiing, so our paths literally do not cross."

I`m not sure I enjoy watching Suzanna compete.

I joined the British team members at the runout, and Todd handed me his binoculars.

"Just stand over there if you`re going to ski with her. You`re bloody dangerous to be close to."

She came a very creditable fourth, and everyone, including Todd Stewart, was delighted with her performance.

"You wait, next season I`ll be regularly on the podium," she declared triumphantly.

We were getting ready for dinner when she dropped the bombshell. She was staring into a mirror about to fit her earrings.

"I`ve decided. . .after we are married. . . I`m going to do the Ladies` Downhill. Judging by my recent experience, I think I could do well with fewer gates to navigate, and skiing that extra distance."

She turned towards me.

"That`s if you agree, of course."

"What, accept you`re going to ski in the Ladies`

Downhill?"

"No, idiot, if you agree to marry me!"

"Give me time to think about it. . .OK, I`ve thought about it. . .of course I agree!"

I moved swiftly across the room and took her in my arms.

"But I`m going to propose properly, and choose the moment," I declared as I bent to kiss her.

EPILOGUE

In the complex on the Black Sea, Leoni Tupolev was standing before a wall of glass staring at the scene on the far promontory.

"I don`t want to know the details, but you have done well, Alexei. Still, I expected nothing less."

He tapped the glass with a finger. "Do you know, I can stand here for hours sometimes, just taking in the view. Now it will soon be restored, it will help me again to meditate on the demanding aspects of life," remarked the President.

He walked back to his desk.

"So, let us talk of your next task. I want you to tell the contractors that they will be paid to take it down. They can remove whatever they wish from the site. The balance will come from your over-generous expenses."

"What! It will cost millions of rubles!" exclaimed Sokolov.

The President smiled. "I jest, Alexei. Like you used to. Just inform the supposed owner of this place the amount to be withdrawn from the mutual account, to preserve our unrestricted view."

He returned to the window to gaze intently at the vista, adding.

"These things are important to me, you know."

●●●

AUTHOR'S NOTES

Although `Ride The Mountain` is a work of fiction, at its core is a sensitive issue which aroused widespread condemnation in Russia. It is the large Italianate-style residence at Gelendzhik Krasnodar Krai, north of Sochi on the Black Sea, built for the President.

It was reported to have cost between six hundred million and a billion dollars, which internal sources suggest had been siphoned off from funds destined for medical projects.

Though a popular leader, at the time, it reflected badly on Vladimir Putin. Particularly, when pictures, taken by a building worker, appeared on the WikiLeaks website.

The media fuelled the flames: to arrest the avalanche of remarks by disgruntled citizens, the complex was seemingly sold to Alexander Ponomarenko, a Russian businessman. He claims the property is now his holiday home. Thus, there is a thread running through the novel touching upon those who serve the fictional President of The Russian Federation

Moreover, I have also included the Bratva, Russia's Mafia, in the narrative, for they also play a role in the telling of the tale.

These two elements form the background to the novel which focuses on the world of professional skiers — notably those who participate in alpine events such as the

Downhill and Super G races.

I seek the forgiveness of those purist athletes who regard the timing of certain major events as sacrosanct. I have taken the bold step of tinkering with the dates and locations of several championships. Thus, the story unfolds in favour of the lead characters and allows the narrative to flow.

Patrick Gooch – 2023

About The Author

Patrick Gooch has enjoyed a varied and interesting career. He studied History of Art, and lectured at the Central School of Art and Design in London. However, marketing has long been his main occupation; and in this role he has worked for a number of international companies.

In recent years, Patrick was appointed chief executive of a Spanish government trade council, which led to the award of `Commander of Civil Merit` conferred on him by King Juan Carlos.

Thereafter, he joined his wife`s trade development company, working with European senders to the UK as well as exporters from Central and South America.

It was the tedium of long-haul business flights and time spent in impersonal hotel rooms that prompted Patrick to take up writing. Thus far, a number of his novels have been published — most combining fact with fiction, taking a different slant on actual events.

www.blossomspringpublishing.com

Printed in Great Britain
by Amazon